Dungeon Jest

The Ruby of POWER

Written by Andrew Snook
Artwork by Jeff Fowler
Inking by Corey King

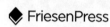 FriesenPress

One Printers Way
Altona, MB R0G0B0,
Canada

www.friesenpress.com

Copyright © 2022 by Andrew Snook
First Edition — 2022

Illustrations by Jeff Fowler

ISBN
978-1-03-912973-3 (Hardcover)
978-1-03-912972-6 (Paperback)
978-1-03-912974-0 (eBook)

1. Fiction, Fantasy, Humorous

Distributed to the trade by The Ingram Book Company

To everyone managing their way through the
COVID-19 coronavirus pandemic,
Those who are surviving,
Those who are thriving,
Those whom we lost,
Those whom we saved,
Those who are saving lives, and
Those who make life worth living,
This one's for you.

How to Play

What you'll need: A pencil, two dice and mad rolling skills.

Encounters: While searching for the Ruby of Power, you will encounter a wide variety of creatures. Some will be friendly, but many will want your head. As a professional Fool, your combat training has been limited to the odd drunken brawl at the local pub, where you were typically pummeled. You begin this quest with **1 Skill** in battle and the ability to do **1 Damage**. Just so we're clear, that sucks. Grab as much gear as you can throughout your adventure and rely on your other skills to help you survive until you feel you've got a fighting chance.

When in battle, you must put your combat skill to the test against your opponent(s). Before combat begins, you must decide which weapon you will be using (if you have one). Once combat begins, roll 1 die and add it to your current Skill points. Then roll 1 die and add it to your opponent's total Skill points. Whoever has the highest total wins that battle round and deals their **Damage** total to their opponent. That damage total is removed from that creature or person's total **Health**. This process continues until either you or your opponent reaches zero health. If your health drops to zero, you have been slain and will need to re-start the game from the beginning.

All ties during a battle round should be re-rolled.

Here's an example:

Let's set our statistics as follows:

STULTY (PLAYER)   SKILL: 2   DAMAGE: 2   HEALTH: 10

ENCOUNTER!

GOBLIN   SKILL: 2   DAMAGE: 1   HEALTH: 5

Let's begin combat by rolling a die for Stulty and the Goblin.

Stulty: Goblin:

Stulty rolled a 3. So, when combined with his 2 Skill points, Stulty has rolled a total of 5. The Goblin rolled a 1. So, when combined with its 2 Skill points, it has rolled a total of 3. This means Stulty won this round of combat and deals 2 Damage to the Goblin, reducing its Health from 5 to 3. Continue this process until one of you reaches 0 Health, vanquishing your opponent.

Health: When you begin your quest, you must roll for your total Health points. Roll 1 die and add 15. That is your total health. When you receive damage throughout your quest, your health does not regenerate. You will need to rely on items you discover on your journey to help restore your health. Keep on the lookout for potions that heal wounds or food items that offer health bonuses when consumed. But beware, an item can have more than one application, so choose to consume them wisely.

Laughter: You are one of the most talented jesters to ever grace the Kingdom of Opulentos. While your jokes and silly high jinks greatly amused the Royal Family, they equally annoyed many members of the Royal Court. You can expect similar reactions in the Labyrinth of the Minotaur. Use the power of laughter to charm angry beasts and avoid unnecessary encounters. To obtain your Laughter score to begin the quest, roll 1 die then add 1 to the total to a maximum score of 5.

Luck: Sometimes Skill, Health and Laughter won't be enough to persevere. Sometimes, you'll simply need a little luck. To obtain your Luck score to begin the quest, roll 1 die to the total to a maximum score of 5.

Allies: When encountering the creatures that reside inside the Labyrinth of the Minotaur, there's a possibility that you will befriend one of these creatures. If you obtain an Ally, that individual will offer a bonus to one of your attributes while they accompany you. During combat, if your Health is dangerously low, you can opt to sacrifice your Ally to prevent taking a round of combat damage. If you sacrifice an Ally in this manner, you must remove their bonus from your attributes.

Stats Sheet

Skill:

Luck:

Laughter:

Damage:

Health:

Allies:

Items:

Battle Sheet

Labyrinth Loot

Boar Meat: Replenish up to 5 lost Health (one use)
Bronze Sword: +2 Damage, +2 Skill (Weapon, one-handed)
Centaur's Pitchfork: +2 Damage, +1 Skill (Weapon, two-handed)
Elixir of Healing: Replenish all lost Health (one use)
Harpy Egg: Replenish up to 5 lost Health (one use)
Heart-Shaped Necklace: +1 Luck (Permanent)
Ice Breaker: +3 Damage, +3 Skill (Weapon, one-handed)
Iron Shield: −1 Damage received from all attacks (Armour)
Mini Slingshot: Deduct 1 Health from opponent before start of combat
Octopus Ink: Throw at opponent to give them −1 Skill for duration of combat (one use)
Potion of Healing: Replenish up to 6 lost Health (one use)
Red Apple: Replenish up to 3 lost Health (one use)
Ring of Defence: −1 Damage received from all attacks (Permanent)
Rusty Dagger: +1 Damage, +1 Skill
Silver Dagger: +1 Damage, +2 Skill (+2 Damage against Vampries, Zombies and Skeletons)
Slime Cupcake: Replenish up to 3 lost Health, then try not to barf (one use)
The Nutcracker: +4 Damage, +4 Skill (Weapon, two-handed)
Wand of Brambles: Prevent all damage from one attack each combat
War Hammer: +3 Damage, +1 Skill (Weapon, two-handed)
Wooden Club: +2 Damage, +1 Skill (Weapon, one-handed)
Vial of Healing: Replenish up to 3 lost Health (one use)

Keep a lookout for any additional special items along your journey

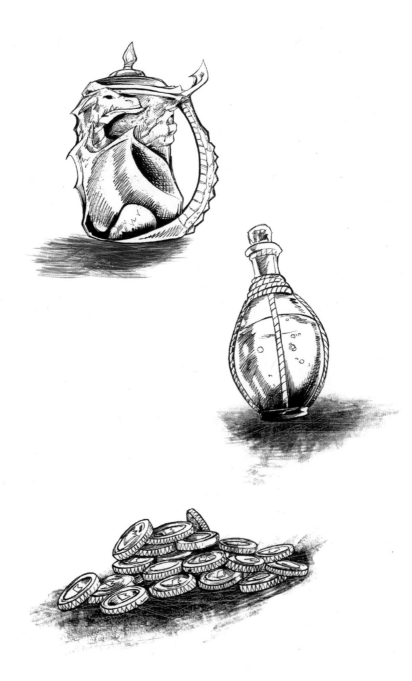

The Beginning

In the Kingdom of Opulentos, there are many snorts and giggles to be had. It has been a realm of laughter and good tidings for many years. King and Queen Opulentos are always in good spirits, and those feelings are passed down throughout the entire kingdom. One could argue that it has been the happiest kingdom for many years. And what is the cause for those tidings of joy? Why you, of course!

As the noble conjurer of the kingdom's ha-has and ho-hos, you, Stultus Insanis Rusticus (or "Stulty," as you are known throughout the kingdom) have lived your life with one purpose: to entertain the Royal Family. The happiness you have brought the kingdom has made you the most popular Fool in the realm. That is, until now...

1

After yet another successful performance for King and Queen Opulentos, you fumble your way out of the Great Hall towards your quarters when you are stopped by Lady Penelope, lady-in-waiting to Princess Nerida.

"Noble Fool, the Princess demands your presence in her chambers for some private entertainment. You must make your way there, post-haste," Lady Penelope says.

If you respond:

- ◆ "Of course, my lady. I shall head there with great haste to bring much-needed joy to my honourable Princess." Turn to 52.

- ◆ "Kiss my pantaloons, you snaggle-toothed buzzard! 'Tis time for mutton, ale and the ogling of fine wenches. I shall not be denied my most carnal desires!" Turn to 75.

2

"Did you ever hear the one about the lusty maiden and the minotaur?" You ask the creatures, who all stare at you confused. "She fell in love with him because he was always horny!"

The creatures lower their weapons and burst into laughter with much hooting and hollering.

"Well sssssspoken," says the lizardman. "Are you the dwarf's new minion?"

You nod to the lizardman. The orcs and goblins go back to their training. The lizardman points you to a wooden door on the opposite side of the room. You walk across the training area and enter the next room. Turn to 150.

3

As you step into the harpy's lair, you accidentally slip on a pile of bird droppings and crash onto the floor. The noise startles the harpy, awakening the creature from its slumber. The harpy watches you with its talons out, ready to shred you to pieces. If you:

- ◆ Draw your weapon and prepare to defend yourself, turn to 108.
- ◆ Offer the harpy a gift, turn to 77.
- ◆ Attempt to run away, turn to 270.
- ◆ Drink your **Potion of Invisibility**, turn to 27.

4

You land on your feet, inches away from a muscular, lizard-like creature, who stands at least ten feet tall. The creature's rancid odour nearly knocks you off your feet. You take a few steps backwards as the monster snarls at you. The lizardman is wielding a large war hammer in its hands. You think carefully about your next move.

- ◆ If you say nothing in response and try to walk around him, turn to 182.

- ◆ If you decide to introduce yourself and explain why you are here, turn to 295.

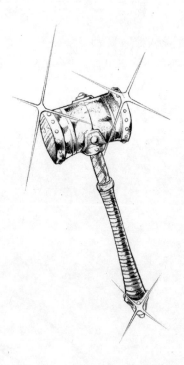

5

The imp scratches its head, looking confused and curious.

"Last part is interesting, but Master Gore will not part with great ruby so you can hit someone with it. Have you brought items to trade?"

You dig through your **Inventory** and pull out:

- ◆ **Mouldy Cheese**, turn to 99.

- ◆ **Harpy Egg**, turn to 153.

- ◆ **Icy Heart**, turn to 86.

- ◆ If you refuse to trade and use the **Wand of Meteor Showers** to crush the dragon and imp with massive space rocks, turn to 271.

- ◆ If you offer nothing and request entrance, turn to 292.

6

You make your way through the tunnel until you encounter a dead end. There are two chains in front of you hanging from the rocky wall. Inscribed on the wall above the left chain are the words, "Don't make the right decision." Above the right chain are the words, "Don't get left behind."

- ◆ If you pull the left chain, turn to 213.
- ◆ If you pull the right chain, turn to 13.

7

The pole just grazes you. Lose **1 Health**. Now, where do you go?

- ◆ If you step back onto your previous panel, then go north, turn to 180.
- ◆ If you decide to step on the panel in front of you, turn to 282.

8

The Twiggle giggles from your silly response.

"Oh Fool, you will need much more than funny words if you expect to escape this place alive. You will need to defeat the minotaur known as Gore, Master of the Labyrinth."

The Twiggle's hand begins to glow and a thorny stick grows from her hand. It emits a warm, green glow. She hands it to you. Add the **Wand of Brambles** to your **Inventory**.

"This will help protect you on your journey," the Twiggle says, before disappearing back into the soil of the grove.

You continue your walk through the grove. Turn to 14.

9

While climbing down through the trap door, you feel icy cold air fill your chest causing your lungs to burn slightly. Your breath becomes visible as you plant your feet on a smooth and slippery surface. You grip the side of the cavern to hold your balance. It is cold to the touch. Raising your lantern, you realize the walls of the cavern are completely covered in ice. As you carefully walk down the frozen corridor, you see the bodies of fellow adventurers encased in icy tombs. You halt your progress entirely when you encounter a massive block of ice blocking your path. Inside the ice stands a large figure that is difficult to make out. You notice a deep crack running through the centre of the ice block.

- If you attempt to break the ice and free the creature, turn to 144.

- If you ignore the frozen creature and continue down the tunnel, turn to 208.

10

You were struck with a curse spell. Lose **1 Luck**. After throwing your own curse words back at the witch, you follow a path leading out of the dungeon. Turn to 19.

11

You beg their forgiveness, apologizing for mistaking them for insects. The leader appears moved by your sincerity.

"Well, I suppose our bugshell armour could give us that appearance," Thorax says. "We shall free you from your bonds this one time, but we do not want to see you ever again. Begone!"

The Bugglebees cut your bonds. You rise to your feet and continue down the tunnel. Turn to 6.

"Halt, Fool!" the taller guard yells.

You ignore his warning and continue to ride away. An arrow flies through the air and strikes you firmly in the buttocks. You scream from the pain and fall off of your horse. Lose **2 Health**. The royal guards ride over to you with their weapons drawn.

"Try that again and you won't have to wait until the labyrinth to meet your end!" the dwarf says as he dismounts, walks over and pulls the arrow from your hiney. You howl in pain. Lose **1 Health**.

You get up, rubbing your sore bottom, mount your horse and continue towards the labyrinth. Turn to 140.

13

You grab the chain and pull it with all of your might. The floor gives way underneath your feet and you slide down a steep, smooth tunnel. You try to grasp the sides of the tunnel but there is a smelly, greasy substance preventing you from getting a proper grip. You quickly come to the end of the tunnel, flying into the air towards piles of hay next to large stalagmites. Make a **Luck** roll.

◆ If you succeed, turn to 49.

◆ If you fail, turn to 266.

14

At the end of the grove is a magic portal. Finding no other way to continue your journey, you run and jump into the portal. Make a **Luck** roll.

- ◆ If you succeed, turn to 4.
- ◆ If you fail, turn to 176.

15

You bang on the door with your fist and wait for a response. The door opens and a harpy attacks you with its talons. Lose **2 Health**. Turn to 108.

16

"Well done, Fool!" the dwarven guard yells as he walks over and slaps you on the back. "I expected you to flee like a coward. You have surprised me with your bravery."

While riding towards the labyrinth, the dwarf pulls a vial out of his pocket and hands it to you. He says that it is a **Potion of Invisibility** and that you should save it for avoiding a dangerous encounter. There is only enough for one dose. When used it will render you invisible for one minute. Add it to your **Inventory**. Turn to 245.

17

You punt the harpy in the head with your foot. It jumps to its feet, angered that its sleep was disturbed. Turn to 108.

18

The pitchfork misses you and lands in a pile of hay. You pick it up and add it to your **Inventory**. The centaur curses you as you make your way past him down the stone path. Turn to 168.

19

As you make your way out of the dungeon, you encounter an orc who unsheathes its weapon and prepares to attack.

- ◆ If you pull out your weapon and prepare to defend yourself, turn to 223.
- ◆ If you try to offer the orc a bribe, turn to 296.

20

The lizardman hisses at you in response to your threat and attacks. Turn to 130.

21

The cyclops smiles and blushes from your compliment. He offers you a cupcake and shuffles you out the door so he can return to decorating his baked goods. Add the **Slimy Cupcake** to your **Inventory**. You make your way back to the main hall and explore the other hallway. Turn to 87.

22

You tell the Bugglebees your classic joke about an archbishop, a dragon and a mouse who walk into a pub together. You quickly have them laughing hysterically.

"Ha! Hilarious, giant!" Thorax says. "You have brought my people more chuckles then we have had in a very long time."

Thorax frees you from your bonds as you explain your quest to him. Turn to 88.

23

You and the harpy exchange long, cautious stares as you open the trap door and descend further into the labyrinth. Turn to 9.

24

You hand the orc all of your gold. Remove it from your **Inventory**.

- ◆ If you had 5 or more gold pieces, turn to 109.
- ◆ If you had less than 5 gold pieces, turn to 62.

25

The Queen cries out for the Royal Guard in response to your explanation. Two large armoured and well-armed men enter the room and look in horror at your exposed twig and berries in close proximity to the Princess. One of the men slaps you with the back of his iron gauntlet, causing you to drop to the floor and hit the back of your head. The two men then grab your ankles and drag you to the Great Hall. Your bare buttocks suffer a nasty friction burn. Turn to 100.

26

The minotaur charges at you and roars, "I shall tear you limb from limb!"

ENCOUNTER!

GORE   SKILL: 3   DAMAGE: 3   HEALTH: 13

If you are victorious, turn to 252.

27

You scramble through your sack, find the **Potion of Invisibility** and drink it. Remove it from your **Inventory**. The harpy, surprised by your disappearance, begins to look around its lair for you. You notice a trap door in its lair. You quietly open the hatch while the harpy's back is turned and slip down further into the labyrinth. Turn to 9.

28

The armour and weapons are too heavy for you, but you find a gold ring. Add the **Ring of Defence** to your **Inventory**.

- ◆ If you try to sneak past the dwarf through the western door, turn to 134.

- ◆ If you attempt to sneak past the dwarf through the northern door, turn to 82.

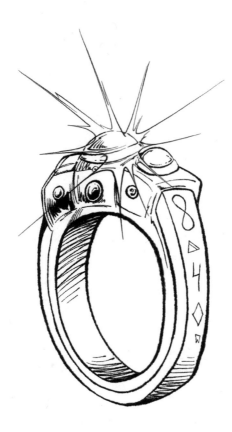

29

You show the pair of eyes the **Icy Heart**. The eyes widen and you hear the door unlock. It opens and a pale hand gestures for you to step into the darkness. As you enter the room, the creature lights a torch, which brightens the room. It is filled with a wide variety of odd knick-knacks displayed on barrels, wooden shelves and tables. The creature standing before you is a vampire with the appearance of an undead middle-aged man. He has pale skin and a protruding tummy. He is wearing a green tunic with the words "DUNGEON CON" sewn into the chest of the garment.

"Let me see that heart!" the creature demands, speaking in a condescending tone.

You hand him the Icy Heart and he inspects it thoroughly. He looks at you approvingly, offering you a fang-filled grin.

"A heart from an Icy Kell in near-mint condition. This will be a great addition for my collection. I have a few duplicate items amongst my treasures that I would be willing to part with for this object. Which one of these would you like in return?" he asks.

- ◆ If you choose a **Bag of Orc Teeth**, turn to 70.

- ◆ If you choose a **Beaker of Octopus Ink**, turn to 115.

- ◆ If you choose an **Elixir of Health**, turn to 204.

30

The royal guards each battle one of the goblins, leaving you with the final creature to slay.

ENCOUNTER!

GOBLIN   **SKILL:** 1   **DAMAGE:** 1   **HEALTH:** 4

If you are victorious, turn to 93.

31

The creature raises its massive icy fists, preparing to crush you, as you pull out your juggling balls. Make a **Laughter** roll.

- ◆ If you succeed, turn to 74.
- ◆ If you fail, turn to 63.

32

You slip out the door into the hallway. On the wall in front of you is a portrait of a minotaur, standing over a fallen adventurer. Congratulations, you have entered the Palace of the Minotaur! The hallway leading south goes to a door with a sign that reads, "KITCHEN, KEEP OUT!" The hallway leading north is unmarked.

◆ If you choose to enter the kitchen, turn to 58.

◆ If you choose to enter the hallway to the north, turn to 283.

33

"Sod off! I just didn't want to clean up the mess. Disturbing my hay piles is bad enough. I don't need the challenge of trying to get blood out of it as well," the centaur says.

If you offer to try to pick the lock on his chains, turn to 198.

If you choose to leave the centaur and follow the stone path, turn to 168.

34

The light from the sun quickly disappears as you make your way into the dark and damp cavern. A few minutes into exploring you encounter the skeleton of an unlucky adventurer, sitting with its back against a cavern wall. The skeleton is holding a rusty key in its bony fist.

- ◆ If you try to remove the key from its grasp, turn to 123.

- ◆ If you try to remove the skeleton's head to use as a puppet, turn to 247.

- ◆ If you leave the key and continue on your journey, turn to 281.

35

A set of stone steps leading upwards takes up most of this room. You can hear beautiful music being played on the second floor. You climb the stairs to look for the source of the wonderful sounds. Turn to 89.

36

You take three balls out from a satchel and begin to juggle.

"These are not the balls I want in my face, Fool," Princess Nerida says shortly before pulling your tights down to your ankles.

You drop the balls as you attempt to steady yourself. The Princess then pulls you on top of her for a different type of entertainment. But before you can begin, Queen Opulentos enters the Princess' private chambers. Upon seeing you lying atop of her daughter with your buttocks in full view she screams, "Have you gone mad, Fool? Get your filthy hands off my daughter!"

If you respond:

- ◆ "My Queen, the Princess demanded my pound of flesh. But I assure you, I only came here to play with my balls." Turn to 25.

- ◆ "Do not fret, my Queen. I can have my dirty bits ready for you shortly after I'm done with the Princess. I only ask for twenty winks, a tall ale and a plate of mutton, you lusty old tart." Turn to 145.

37

The woman's shackle opens up and she cackles as she exits the cell. You watch as she runs over to a chest in the dungeon and retrieves a broom and a purple potion.

"You have been an excellent minion, as useful as any of my flying monkeys. And so, take this as a reward," the witch says as she tosses you the purple potion. "When your doom is certain, drink this and you shall be saved."

Add an **Elixir of Healing** to your **Inventory**. You hear someone approaching.

"Sounds like the guard is coming back, dearie. Time for me to go," the witch says as she hops onto her broom and flies through the sewage tunnel you entered the dungeon from.

The footsteps from the guard are getting closer. With no time to hide, you draw your weapon and prepare to face the guard. Turn to 188.

38

The imp raises its bony hand in the air and says, "Dinner time!" before snapping its fingers. Cuddles opens its mouth and releases a massive burst of fire, turning you into a crispy critter. Your quest has ended.

39

The cyclops takes the onion but doesn't appear overly impressed. He tosses you 1 gold coin. Remove the **Mouldy Onion** from your **Inventory**.

- ◆ If you choose to offer him another item, return to 293.
- ◆ Otherwise, turn to 298.

40

The dragon and imp both burst into laughter. The dragon rolls on its back, accidentally crushing the imp. You decide to sneak past the dragon into the courtyard before it realizes what it has done. Turn to 69.

41

Excited to take your first step to the other side of the path, you don't notice the floor give way until you are descending into the darkness.

- ◆ Make a **Luck** roll. If you succeed, turn to 219.
- ◆ If you fail, turn to 172.

42

With your final blow, you pierce the monster's body, releasing a pile of gold coins, killing the creature. Add 100 gold pieces to your **Inventory**. After collecting the treasure, you leave the dungeon and continue on your quest. Turn to 212.

43

A large shard of ice flies into your chest and impales you against an icy wall of the cavern. You begin to lose consciousness as you watch your blood pour out onto the icy floor forming a steaming red puddle. Your quest has ended.

44

"Nice try, monster, but your journey ends here," Thorax says as he motions for his soldiers to take aim.

The last thing you see is a sea of tiny stones flying towards your face. Your quest has ended.

45

- ◆ Make a **Luck** roll. If you succeed, turn to 129.
- ◆ If you fail, turn to 166.

46

"That sapphire is an uncommon jewel at best. Keep your blue rock for a less sophisticated collector," the voice says in a condescending tone.

- ◆ If you want to offer another gift, return to 229.
- ◆ If not, you decide to return to the sewer and try your luck jumping into the stream. Turn to 196.

47

ENCOUNTER!

OGRE   SKILL: 2   DAMAGE: 4   HEALTH: 13

If you are victorious, you search the creature's remains and place the **Gold Key** in your **Inventory**. Ascend the stairs to explore the second floor of the palace. Turn to 89.

48

You throw the **Vial of Acid** at the Icy Kell. Make a **Luck** roll.

- ◆ If you succeed, turn to 55.
- ◆ If you fail, turn to 83.

49

You land in a pile of hay next to a sharp stalagmite. A male centaur approaches you and pulls you from the hay pile.

"Thank the Gods, you landed in the hay!" the centaur says. "I thought for certain as I watched you hurdle towards me that you were going to land buttocks first onto a rocky spike. It would have taken me ages to clean up the mess, not to mention all the hay you would have ruined!"

You brush yourself off and adjust your coxcomb as you take in your surroundings. You notice that the centaur is chained at the hoof to a large boulder. Behind him is a stone path. If you reply:

- ◆ "Great thanks to you, noble centaur! Your worry of the health of my buttocks is greatly appreciated." Turn to 33.

- ◆ "Back off horse-man, I need no help from one of nature's abominations!" Turn to 149.

- ◆ "Allow me to try to remove those chains, noble creature," turn to 198.

- ◆ If you choose to say nothing and continue down the stone path behind him. Turn to 168.

50

You toss the **Bag of Orc Teeth** to the guard, who opens the bag and screams in terror upon inspecting the contents inside. In fear for his teeth, the orc drops the bag, scattering its contents all over the cavern floor. He then turns away from you and flees. Remove the **Bag of Orc Teeth** from your **Inventory**. You continue down the path on your quest. Turn to 212.

51

You look around the room and see a large nest made mostly of straw, as well as a small wooden chest and a trap door on the floor. Inside the harpy's nest you find a **Harpy Egg**. Add it to your **Inventory**.

- ◆ If you choose to search the wooden chest, turn to 73.

- ◆ If not, you open up the trap door and descend further into the labyrinth. Turn to 9.

52

After making your way to Princess Nerida's private chambers, you stop at the large oak double-doors and announce your presence.

If you yell:

- ◆ "My Princess, your noble Fool is here to fill your soul with joy and laughter." Turn to 125.

- ◆ "Prepare your booty for fun-filled jiggles and giggles, my lovely Princess!" Turn to 210.

53

You search the body but find nothing of interest. The meat cleaver the creature attacked you with is too heavy to wield effectively as a weapon. The kitchen floor is covered in smashed cupcakes. While searching the mess, you are able to find one cupcake decorated with slime and toad eyes that survived. Add the **Slimy Cupcake** to your **Inventory**. You hear footsteps approaching. The noise from the battle may have alerted the palace guards. You decide to leave through a door in the back of the kitchen and continue searching the palace for the Ruby of Power. Turn to 132.

54

You stumble around the room and shake your jester's staff but fail to get any laughs from the creatures. The monsters quickly lose patience and attack, overwhelming you and hacking your body into pieces. Your quest has ended.

55

The vial shatters upon impact with the Icy Kell's face. The monster screams in agony momentarily before its face is melted away. The creature falls dead at your feet. Its body cracks apart and splinters into little pieces. You search the remains and discover an **Icy Heart** and add it your **Inventory** before continuing down the icy corridor. Turn to 208.

56

Congratulations! You have vanquished Gore, ruler of the labyrinth. You step over the minotaur's fallen body and walk into his treasure room. To the victor goes the spoils! Turn to 252.

57

The lock is extremely difficult to pick. You attempt a **Luck** roll.

- ◆ If you roll a 6, you successfully pick the lock. Turn to 131.

- ◆ If you fail, return to 197 and choose another option.

58

As you open the back door of the kitchen, you are met with a sweet aroma, followed by the scent of pickled fish. The kitchen has a crudely constructed stone oven, several tables and shelves housing ingredients. A large, muscular cyclops wearing a chef's hat and apron is standing in front of you. He is holding a tray of slimy cupcakes.

"You not allowed in here! What you want?" the cyclops asks.

- ◆ If you draw your weapon and attack, turn to 67.

- ◆ If you explain that you are a merchant looking to sell rare ingredients, turn to 293.

59

You come to the entrance of a small palace. The clay and stone walls of the palace are adorned with bones from a variety of creatures. The steps leading up to the entrance are carpeted in dragon scales. Your nostrils are filled with the smell of sulphur and charred flesh. As you make your way up the steps, you can hear booming footsteps drawing near. A large green dragon steps out from the entrance of the courtyard. While wondering if you're about to be its next meal, a small brown imp flutters out from behind the dragon and lands next to the creature to greet you.

"Welcome! I am the great Stickywings, overlord of all who are imp," the creature says. "Tell me, what brings you to my Master's lair?"

If you respond:

- ◆ "I am on a great quest to obtain the Ruby of Power. I must speak with your master and request the fabled jewel from him, so I may bring it to King and Queen Opulentos and toss it at their fat heads for sending me here." Turn to 5.

- ◆ "Silence, you foul, flying bug-like demon, before I swat you away like the pathetic pest you are!" Turn to 38.

- ◆ "I am the greatest Fool in all the land, here to bring great amusement to Master Gore. Allow me the opportunity to make you snort and giggle." Turn to 120.

60

As the dwarf relieves himself, you decide to turn and charge your steed at the archer. Before you are able to get within striking distance, the soldier takes aim and strikes you with two arrows in your chest. You fall off your horse and collapse onto the ground. The guards leave you to rot and make their way back to the castle to inform King and Queen Opulentos of your death. Your quest has ended.

61

"I'm afraid we know not where the fabled jewel is located, but we wish you the best of luck on your journey," Thorax says.

You curse under your breath and continue down the tunnel. Turn to 6.

62

The orc takes your gold but is offended at the paltry sum. Remove all gold pieces from your **Inventory**. He screams a battle cry and attacks. Turn to 223.

63

While attempting to juggle, you slip on the ice and fall, acciden-tally tossing the balls in the air and bouncing them off the face of the Icy Kell. The frozen giant roars and grabs you with one of its monstrous hands. You smile at the creature, hoping to calm the beast. No such luck. The creature raises its massive fist and brings it down on your skull. Your quest has ended.

64

While entering the next room, you can hear what sounds like loud snoring. You see a large ogre fast asleep, leaning against a set of stone steps leading up to the second floor of the palace. Dangling on his belt you can see a gold key with minotaur horns engraved at the handle.

- ◆ If you would like to attempt to steal the key, turn to 272.

- ◆ Otherwise, you continue up the stairs. Turn to 89.

65

Trying not to soil your pantaloons, you step forwards onto the panel. Silence. Thanking the gods for your good fortune, you step off the panel and continue down the stone path. Turn to 59.

66

You remove two puppets on strings both dressed as fools, and make them run around, stumble and dance for the Princess, but she appears to be unimpressed. Prince Nerida smiles as she takes the puppets from your hands and tosses them to the ground. She then slips your hands underneath her purple satin sheet, placing them on her ample bosom.

"If you want to play with something, Fool, then play with these!" she says.

At that moment, Queen Opulentos enters the Princess' chambers and freezes up as she stares in horror at your desecration of her daughter's innocence.

"Remove your filthy hands from my daughter!" she commands.

If you responded:

- ◆ "My Queen, this is a terrible misunderstanding. When I came to the Princess' chambers, I only planned to play with myself." Turn to 105.

- ◆ "I cannot, my Queen. There is no finer set of dirty pillows in all the land then those I hold now. I look forward to placing my face between them and making magical sounds." Turn to 205.

67

ENCOUNTER!

CYCLOPS   SKILL: 3   DAMAGE: 4   HEALTH: 13

You catch the monster by surprise and get one free chance to strike him. Afterwards, deduct the damage from his total **Health**. The cyclops then picks up a large meat cleaver and you continue the battle as normal. If you survive, turn to 53.

68

After defeating the zombies, you decide to hold your breath and search their bloated, rotting corpses. You discover a golden **Heart-Shaped Necklace**. You add the necklace to your **Inventory** and decide on your next move.

- ◆ If you choose to explore the path to the north, turn to 235.

- ◆ If you decide to jump into the stream and follow the current, turn to 196.

69

In the courtyard of the palace stands a large gold statue of a mino-taur holding a two-handed battle axe. Dozens of rusty weapons and pieces of armour are littered at the base of the statue.

- ◆ If you choose to scavenge through the pile to look for something useful, turn to 261.

- ◆ If you prefer to enter the palace, turn to 201.

70

"An intelligent choice," the vampire says. "Orcs are fearful of losing their chompers. Use them to intimidate a young orc, or to make a fancy necklace."

You thank the vampire for the transaction and ask if you may pass through his lair to continue on your quest. The vampire motions to a door on the other side of his lair.

"Now leave, before I decide to have you for my next meal. I am growing parched and will require sustenance soon," he says.

You nod and quickly make your way through the vampire's home, moving deeper into the lair of the minotaur. Turn to 244.

The larger ice shards miss you by mere inches and impact against the cavern walls. A few of the smaller shards slice open your legs and arms. Lose **2 Health**. A large, glowing blue translucent creature now stands before you. The liquid you poured into the ice burned a whole through the creature's chest. Its eyes open up momentarily, shortly before the creature falls to the floor and shatters into a thousand pieces. You search the remains of the icy giant and find what appears to be its heart amongst the rubble. You add the **Icy Heart** to your **Inventory** then continue down the frozen path. Turn to 208.

72

You take aim and bring your club down towards the spike. Unfortunately, you miss and strike the centaur's hoof. The centaur screams in pain then winds up and kicks you with enough force to toss you back into a hay pile. Lose **3 Health**. The centaur then tramples your Wooden Club, smashing it into pieces, and tosses away your iron spike. Remove both from your **Inventory**. After catching your breath, you decide it would be best to leave the centaur alone and continue down the stone path. Turn to 168.

73

You find a **Small Sapphire**, **Elixir of Health**, and a **Vial of Green Liquid**. Add them to your inventory. You notice a trap door leading further into the labyrinth. Cautiously, you slowly open the door and climb down further into the darkness. Turn to 9.

74

You dance around the cavern, juggling your balls while singing a catchy tune about King Opulentos and the mysterious rash he woke up with after a night with his serving wench. The Icy Kell claps its massive hands together and lets out a booming laugh that causes the whole cavern to vibrate. When you complete your performance, you bow to the icy giant. The creature points to your juggling balls and reaches out its frozen hands.

- ◆ If you give him the juggling balls, turn to 214.

- ◆ If you refuse, turn to 279.

75

Lady Penelope did not respond well to your rejection. Shortly after your brief encounter, you are met by members of the King's Royal Guard, who grab you by the arms and drag you back into the Great Hall. Turn to 200.

76

"You dare mock me, mortal! Prepare to face thy doom!" the vampire yells as it unsheathes its sword. You step back and prepare to defend yourself.

ENCOUNTER!

VAMPIRE   SKILL: 2   DAMAGE: 2   HEALTH: 12

If the creature's health falls below 5, you may choose to stop the battle.

- ♦ If you choose to stop the battle, turn to 183.
- ♦ If you decide to fight to the death and win, turn to 253.

77

You hastily rummage through your sack.

- ♦ If you pull out a **Mouldy Onion**, turn to 81.
- ♦ If you offer 5 gold pieces, turn to 165.
- ♦ If you retrieve a **Mouldy Cheese**, turn to 259.

78

You shift your body to the right and continue to pick up momentum as you approach a light at the end of the tunnel. Your body is fired into the air and all you can see on your way down is a bright pool of molten lava. You curse the King and Queen as you hurdle towards your impending doom. Your quest has ended.

79

You yank the pointy utensil from your buttocks and fling it at the ogre yelling, "Fork you!"

The fork bounces off its forehead onto the floor. The creature becomes enraged and jumps onto the table, raising its massive stone club. Before you have a chance to defend yourself, the ogre's weapon descends on your skull and everything goes dark. Your quest has ended.

80

You pick up the Ruby of Power and toss it at Gore's feet. It shatters on impact and explodes in a white-hot blaze of fire, turning the minotaur to ash. You have defeated Gore but have destroyed the Ruby of Power in the process. You will never be able to return to the Kingdom of Opulentos. You have failed in your quest.

81

You hold up the onion and the harpy cocks its head, as if it were saying, *Is that for me?*

Slowly, you place the onion on the ground and roll it towards the harpy, who snatches it up with its talons and takes a big bite of the rotten vegetable. Remove the **Mouldy Onion** from your **Inventory**. Satisfied with your gift, the harpy motions to a trap door in her lair next to her nest. You walk over to the door and open it as the harpy returns to its nest to finish her snack. Descending into the darkness you hear a loud belch from above, followed by snoring. Turn to 9.

82

The dwarf continues to hammer away, not noticing you slip into the north door. Turn to 64.

83

The **Vial of Acid** flies over the creature's shoulder and shatters against a cavern wall, melting the ice. Remove it from your **Inventory**. The giant roars at you and raises its massive fists. Turn to 249.

84

"Calm yourself, my well-endowed friend," you say to the centaur. "Allow me to fill you with laughter using my friends, Snicker and Snort."

You pull out your puppets and make them dance around. The centaur is not amused. He turns his backside to you and drops a steaming pile of leftovers onto the puppets. You curse out the centaur and stomp away towards the stone path. Turn to 168.

85

You snatch an apple from the tree and take a big bite. The crisp apple begins to turn rotten in your mouth. You wretch and spit out a mouthful of maggots. Lose **1 Health**.

"Sssstupid, greedy humanssss," the snake hisses before slithering away.

Roots sprout out of the ground near your feet at a feverish pace, transforming into a creature comprised of branches and thorns. Your disrespectful behaviour has offended the guardian of the grove.

ENCOUNTER!

TWIGGLE   **SKILL:** 3   **DAMAGE:** 2   **HEALTH:** 7

If you win the battle, turn to 238.

86

You remove the **Icy Heart** from your sack and show it to the imp. The creature flies over to you, takes the heart and returns to Cuddles the dragon. Remove the **Icy Heart** from your **Inventory**.

"Yes, this will do nicely," the imp says. "Now, what else have you brought to trade?"

- ◆ If you offer **Mouldy Cheese**, turn to 99.

- ◆ If you offer a **Harpy Egg**, turn to 153.

- ◆ If you use the **Wand of Meteor Showers** to crush the dragon and imp, turn to 271.

- ◆ If you offer them nothing else and request entrance into the palace, turn to 292.

87

The hallway leads to a wooden door. Antique weapons and mounted heads of various creatures hang on the walls. As you get closer to the door, you hear what sounds like grunting, yelling and the clashing of weapons. You are certain that a battle is in progress.

- ◆ If you open the door to investigate further, turn to 275.
- ◆ If you would rather try your luck exploring the other hallway, turn to 239.

88

"We shall help you on your quest, giant," Thorax declares. "How can we be of assistance?"

- ◆ If you ask for the best path to the ancient Ruby of Power, turn to 61.
- ◆ If you request an item to help you on your journey, turn to 138.
- ◆ If you ask for a travelling companion to watch your back, turn to 299.

89

While walking up the staircase, a sweet melody fills your ears. It is reminiscent of a child's lullaby. When you arrive at the top of the stairs you see a massive steel door directly in front of you. To your left, a female naga plays a harp with all four of her arms. She removes one of her hands from the instrument and places a finger on her mouth, signalling you to be silent.

"Shh, the masssster does not want to be disssssturbed," she says. "Sssstate your businesssss."

- ◆ If you have the **Gold Key**, you can explain that you are here to clean his quarters. If this is the case, turn to 257.

- ◆ If you have the **Iron Bracer** in your **Inventory** and want to claim you're delivering it to the master, turn to 224.

- ◆ If you reply, "I am here to bring him much joy and amusement, but I'm sure he's already in good hands my four-armed beauty," turn to 147.

- ◆ If you say, "Don't throw a hisssssssssy fit, my dear. I'm simply here to take the Ruby of Power." Turn to 294.

90

The cyclops sniffs the meat and gives you a big smile. He hands you a **Ring of Defence**. Remove the **Boar Meat** from your **Inventory**.

◆ If you choose to offer him another item, return to 293.

◆ Otherwise, turn to 298.

91

You carefully place the **Iron Spike** into the lock and raise your **Wooden Club**.

"Do not miss, Fool," the centaur warns you.

Make a **Luck** roll.

◆ If you succeed, turn to 114.

◆ If you fail, turn to 72.

92

"Be careful what you ask for, my dirty little Fool!" the Princess says as she begins to crouch down.

At that moment, the Queen enters the Princess' chambers and shrieks in horror.

"What do you think you are doing, Fool? Get away from my daughter!" Queen Opulentos commands.

Princess Nerida steps away from you as two of the Royal Guard enter the room to investigate the Queen's scream.

"Take this foul thing to the Great Hall for judgement!" the Queen commands.

The guards grab your ankles and drag you out of the Princess' chambers. Turn to 100.

93

After a brief, celebratory booty dance, you search the remains of the goblin to find: **5 Gold**, a **Wooden Club** and a **Mouldy Onion**. Add them to **Inventory**. Turn to 16.

94

You place the **Iron Spike** into the crack and use the **Wooden Club** like a hammer. The crack in the ice spreads with every strike. You drive the spike deeper into the ice at a feverish pace as the cold air begins to numb your hands. After twenty strikes, the block of ice cracks open and reveals a monstrous figure apparently made entirely of ice. The Icy Kell begins to emit a glowing blue aura as its eyes slowly open up and focus on you. You hear what sounds like a growl coming from the creature as it begins to walk towards you.

- ◆ If you would like to use an item, turn to 173.

- ◆ If you choose to attack the creature, turn to 249.

95

You open the **Sack of Manure** to show the glowing eyes but trip as you make your way forwards, flinging the foul substance all over the door and into the eyes of the creature. It screams in response. Remove the **Sack of Manure** from your **Inventory**.

"Blech! You shall meet your doom for this insolence!" the creature yells.

The door opens up and you are met by a vampire, who appears to be middle-aged and has a large belly protruding almost out of his green tunic. The tunic has the words "DUNGEON CON" sewn onto the chest of the garment. He is holding a bronze sword.

"Prepare yourself for a duel!" the vampire challenges.

ENCOUNTER!

VAMPIRE   **SKILL:** 2   **DAMAGE:** 2   **HEALTH:** 12

If the creature's health drops below 5, you may choose to stop the battle.

- ◆ If you choose to stop the battle, turn to 183.
- ◆ If you fight him to the death and are victorious, turn to 253.

96

Make a **Laughter** roll.

◆ If you succeed, turn to 8.

◆ If you fail, turn to 159.

97

The cyclops looks at your measly little beans and shakes his head.

◆ If you choose to offer him another item, return to 293.

◆ Otherwise, turn to 298.

98

You walk up to the chest and attempt to open it. Eyes open on the top of the chest, startling you. You stumble backwards. The top of the chest opens up, revealing dozens of sharp teeth. The creature growls and snaps its teeth at you. Raising your weapon, you prepare to defend yourself.

ENCOUNTER!

TREASURE CHOMPER   **SKILL: 1**   **DAMAGE: 2**   **HEALTH: 8**

If you are victorious, turn to 42.

99

The imp begins to drool at the sight of the **Mouldy Cheese**.

"Gimme!" he yells as he flies over to you and snatches it from your hands, then returns to Cuddles the dragon. The imp eats the cheese and lets out a satisfied belch. Remove Mouldy Cheese from your **Inventory**.

"Ah, delicious. Now, what else have you brought to trade?" the imp asks.

- ◆ If you offer a **Harpy Egg**, turn to 153.

- ◆ If you offer the **Icy Heart**, turn to 86.

- ◆ If you use the **Wand of Meteor Showers** to crush the dragon and imp, turn to 271.

- ◆ If you offer them nothing else and request entrance into the palace, turn to 292.

100

The guards shackle you and force you to kneel in front of the royal thrones while you await your fate. An hour later, King and Queen Opulentos enter the Great Hall alongside Dolus Malus, the court wizard, who you have always considered a pompous ass and all-around bad guy. The hall has filled with nobles and servants whom you have often mingled with, mocked, imitated and otherwise vexed.

"Rise, Fool!" the King commands.

As you stand, you notice Dolus Malus grinning and rubbing his hands together, practically bubbling over with anticipation of something to come. Wizards doth sucketh the heftiest of donkey parts.

"You have greatly offended my Queen and attempted to sully my innocent daughter. For this, I should have you locked in the dungeon for the rest of your days," King Opulentos says. "However, after careful consult with the Queen and our loyal advisor, the wise Dolus Malus, we have decided to offer you an opportunity for absolution."

You nod, praying forgiveness will come in any form other than a suicidal run through the Labyrinth of the Minotaur, one of the King's favourite ways to dispatch subjects he dislikes.

"Instead of rotting in the castle dungeon, you shall make your way to the Labyrinth of the Minotaur and retrieve the ancient Ruby of Power," King Opulentos says, as the sounds of dread and laughter fill the Great Hall. "Our bravest knights and adventurers seeking glory for the past two centuries have failed to retrieve the magical jewel. It's believed to be held by the wicked minotaur Gore, who calls the cursed labyrinth his home. Now you, Stultus Insanis Rusticus, shall go on this honoured and ancient quest to honour your King and Queen and bring great prestige to our kingdom."

You curse under your breath as you listen to the people of the court snicker and whisper to each other about your impending doom. Dolus Malus steps forward holding three small sacks.

"Noble Fool, your quest will be a perilous one," Malus says. "You will need to be well equipped if you are to survive your journey and bring back the fabled Ruby of Power. I have enchanted these sacks and filled them each with items that can assist you in your quest. You may choose only one for your journey, so choose wisely."

You're sure he's totally screwing with you – revenge for slipping a spike onto his seat during last year's royal banquet. Malus had to wear a pillow for a month, and you're certain he hasn't forgotten about it.

"Choose, Fool. Let fate guide your hand," he says with a mischievous grin.

Which sack do you choose?

- ◆ Blue: Turn to 158.

- ◆ Purple: Turn to 221.

- ◆ Green: Turn to 240.

101

The spiked pole pierces through your gut, leaving you dangling in the air, skewered like a piece of meat. You are now prepped to be placed over a warm fire for dinner by the next hungry creature that encounters your corpse. Your quest has ended.

102

You pull out a knight puppet and a dragon puppet, which catches Cuddles' attention. The dragon puppet chases the knight puppet on the steps for a few seconds before catching and eating him. You make the knight scream for mercy as it is gobbled up, before finishing with the dragon producing a loud belch. When you finish your puppet show, you look up and see the dragon and imp staring at you. Make a **Laughter** roll.

- ◆ If you succeed, turn to 40.
- ◆ If you fail, turn to 127.

103

Clapping your hands together while singing a catchy tune about a harlot from Hedon that gave villagers "The Devil's Itch," you skip, hop and roll around the Princess' chambers. While you are mid-roll, Princess Nerida places her foot on your chest and stands over you, allowing a glimpse into her most sacred area.

If you respond:

- ◆ "My Princess, your sacred bush is exposed to my eyes. Shall I call the chamber maiden to fetch you some undergarments, or perhaps, the royal gardener to perform some trimming?" Turn to 170.

- ◆ "I spy with my little eye, something that may be heavenly. Alas, my Princess, this Fool's eyes aren't quite what they used to be. So, I will need a closer look, just to be sure." Turn to 92.

104

You raise your weapon over your head and bring it down with all of your might onto the harpy's skull. The creature awakens but is stunned from the attack. Fuelled by fear, you repeatedly bash the harpy's skull until it stops thrashing about in its nest. You have successfully killed the creature, but the **Wooden Club** was badly cracked and splintered during the attack. Remove it from your **Inventory**. Turn to 51.

105

The Queen looks at you with disgust then calls for the Royal Guard. Two armed men enter the room and await further commands.

"Take this disgusting wretch to the Great Hall for judgement," the Queen commands.

The two guards grab your arms and drag you out of Princess Nerida's chambers. Turn to 100.

106

You begin to sing and dance while clapping your hands and running around a hay pile. You sing:

> *There was a centaur locked up in chains,*
> *Yearning for freedom caused him great pain.*
> *Along came a Fool, who offered a song,*
> *To the sad creature and his enormous dong!*

The centaur laughs from your serenade.

"Very amusing, Fool. Alas, I am still a prisoner in this labyrinth," the centaur says.

- ◆ If you try to free him from his chains, turn to 198.

- ◆ Otherwise, you wish the centaur the best of luck and continue down the stone path behind him. Turn to 168.

107

The lizardman bursts into hysterical laughter at your ridiculous threat. He walks over to you and gives you a hearty slap on the back and tells you to proceed down the path.

"Remember to follow the path of NENEN, human. It shall keep you safe," the lizard man says as he returns to his post guarding the portal.

You nod, pretending to understand what he's talking about and continue down the path. Turn to 264.

108

ENCOUNTER!

HARPY   SKILL: 2   DAMAGE: 2   HEALTH: 10

If you are victorious, turn to 51.

109

The orc approves of your bribe, pockets the gold and walks past you towards the dungeon. Add +1 to your **Luck** score. You continue down the path on your quest. Turn to 212.

110

Annoyed, the witch curses you for your incompetence. Subtract -1 from your **Luck** score. You find a path leading out of the dungeon and follow it, after offering the witch a few curse words of your own. Turn to 19.

111

Make a **Laughter** roll.

- ◆ If you succeed, turn to 22.
- ◆ If you fail, turn to 44.

112

"Do not worry, my friend. I pick locks the way I make love. 'Tis clumsy and awkward, but quite effective, I assure you!" you tell the centaur.

He chuckles from your comments, causing his leg to shift slightly while you attempt to pick the lock. The centaur's sudden movement caused the lock to make a "click" sound before releasing and falling to the ground. Add **1 Luck**.

The centaur rubs its leg where the chain had sat for so long, then turns his attention to you.

"My name is Gallup. I am in your debt, Fool. I shall accompany you and help you leave this wicked place."

Add **Gallup** to your **Allies** list. He joins your side as you both make your way down the stone path. Turn to 168.

113

As Thorax works on the lock, he accidentally stabs the centaur in the leg. The centaur jumps in response and accidentally crushes Thorax under its hoof. Remove **Thorax** from your **Allies** list. The centaur apologizes for crushing your friend and lowers his head in shame. You pick up Thorax's broken body and bury him in a patch of dirt before leaving the centaur and continuing down a stone path. Turn to 168.

114

You drive the iron spike into the lock with your club with your first strike. The second strike pops the lock open and the centaur is freed from his chains.

"Great thanks to you, Fool. My name is Gallup, and I am in your debt. I shall accompany you and help you leave this accursed place."

Add **Gallup** to your **Allies** list.

You follow Gallup towards the stone path and make your way further into the labyrinth. Turn to 168.

"Ah, an escape artist, are you? This may be of great use to you," the vampire says.

After thanking the vampire for the trade, you request his permission to travel through his chambers so you can continue on your quest. The vampire points to an exit on the far side of his lair.

"Now go, before I decide to have you for a snack!" he says.

You quickly make your way through his lair and move deeper into the Labyrinth of the Minotaur. Turn to 244.

116

You place the **Magic Beans** in a patch of soil near the tree. Remove them from your **Inventory**. The ground opens up and swallows them. Moments later, an enormous beanstalk springs from the soil and grows up into the cavern ceiling, wrapping itself around massive stalactites. Another set of roots begins to grow from the soil near your feet. You take a few steps backwards and watch as the roots form a female figure shaped entirely from thorny branches. It is a Twiggle, a mystical creature best known for being guardians of the natural world.

"You have offered new life to the grove. The Twiggles are grateful," she says. "The evil minotaur, Gore, has corrupted much of this place. Have you come here to stop his tyranny?"

If you respond:

- ◆ "Nice bush, you're making me thorny, baby!" Turn to 96.

- ◆ "Yes, noble guardian of the grove. I intend to take the Ruby of Power, slay the foul man-beast and bring peace to this place." Turn to 128.

117

"Bah! A common item down here. Hardly a collectible," the creature says, scoffing at your gift.

- ◆ If you want to try to offer him a different gift, return to 229.

- ◆ Otherwise, you give up and decide to try your luck at the stream. Turn to 196.

118

The faerie claps her hands together covering you in faerie dust, causing you to sneeze uncontrollably several times. When the sneezing stops, you find yourself just outside the walls to the Royal Palace of Opulentos. Turn to 300.

119

You open the door and a blast of hot air hits you in the face. The majority of the room is taken up by a forge, making the environment swelteringly hot. A dwarf is hard at work, hammering away at a piece of metal, shaping it into a sword. He has not noticed you. You look around the room and see multiple pieces of armour and weapons resting on racks. A minotaur's face is engraved on all the equipment. Congratulations, you have successfully entered the Lair of the Minotaur! There are two doors leading out of the forge.

- ◆ If you choose to sneak by the dwarf and slip out the door to the west, turn to 134.

- ◆ If you try to sneak by the dwarf and leave through the door to the north, turn to 82.

- ◆ If you want to attempt to steal a piece of equipment, turn to 28.

120

"Huzzah, some entertainment!" the imp cries before flying onto Cuddles and taking a seat on the dragon's head. "Amuse us, Fool."

What do you do?

- ◆ If you juggle balls, turn to 290.

- ◆ If you dance and sing, turn to 231.

- ◆ If you perform a puppet show, turn to 102.

121

Attempt a **Luck** roll.

- ◆ If you are successful, turn to 285.

- ◆ If you fail, turn to 199.

122

Your body feels tingly and warm from the spell momentarily, before feeling a searing pain in your head. Your skull is pierced by a small set of antlers that are now part of you. Add +1 to your **Laughter** score. The witch begins to cackle at the sight of you and soon falls to the ground in laughter. You follow a path leading out of the dungeon while picking at your new antlers. Turn to 19.

123

You carefully bend each bony finger back to release the skeleton's hold on the rusted key. After bending back the final finger, you place your hand on the key. At that moment, the skeleton's hand closes and squeezes your hand tightly. The skeleton turns its skull and stares at you with an empty, eerie gaze.

"Thief," it whispers while opening its jaw to reveal its sharp, dagger-like teeth.

You recoil in horror, nearly soiling your pantaloons. As you pull free of its grasp, the skeleton's bony fingers cut your hand. Lose **1 Health**. The skeleton rises to its feet and attacks.

ENCOUNTER!

SKELETON   **SKILL:** 1   **DAMAGE:** 1   **HEALTH:** 6

If you are victorious, turn to 227.

124

You slowly open the door and see a muscular cyclops dressed in a chef's hat and apron. He is busy decorating cupcakes with slime and toad eyes. The cyclops spots you out of the corner of its eye, picks up a large meat cleaver and yells, "You not be in here! Me make cupcakes for Master Gore!"

If you respond:

- ◆ "Sorry to disturb you in the middle of your work, great chef. I couldn't help myself, for the fine aroma of your treats is irresistible." Turn to 21.

- ◆ "Apologies, it smelled like something died in here and I was hoping to loot the corpse. My mistake, carry on." Turn to 232.

- ◆ "Sorry to disturb you, great chef, but I am a merchant of rare ingredients and I have come to offer you my finest items." Turn to 293.

125

Princess Nerida calls for you to enter her chambers and close the door behind you. As you walk into her private bedroom, you are greeted by the Princess, who is dressed in a purple satin sheet tied together at the shoulder. Her long raven black hair flows down onto her ample bosom. Caught off guard by her untraditional garment and exposed skin, you ogle her before you can shift your eyes away.

"I die of boredom. Entertain me, my Fool," the Princess demands as she sits at the end of her bed and smiles mischievously.

What will you do?

- ◆ If you dance, turn to 103.

- ◆ If you decide to juggle balls, turn to 36.

- ◆ If you perform a puppet show, turn to 66.

126

You toss the **Sapphire** at the Icy Kell. The frost giant catches the gem in his massive hand and crushes it into dust. Remove it from your **Inventory**.

- ◆ If you would like to choose another item, turn to 173.

- ◆ Otherwise, turn to 249.

127

"What a splendid idea!" the imp says, as the creature snaps its bony fingers. "Dinner time, Cuddles!"

You attempt to flee, but the dragon opens its mouth and releases a sea of flames incinerating you. Your quest has ended.

128

The Twiggle grabs you and pulls you close to her in a joyous embrace. Her thorns poke you in multiple places. Lose **1 Health**. The creature notices your discomfort and releases her grip on you.

"I am so sorry. I'm just excited you're here to help rid us of the dreaded Gore, Master of the Labyrinth. Please, take my magic wand. It will protect you on your journey. Good luck!" she says before disappearing back into the earth of the grove floor.

Add **Wand of Brambles** to your **Inventory**. You continue your walk through the grove. Turn to 14.

129

You exert all of your energy attempting to pull the jewel out of the mural. It will not budge. While catching your breath, you lean against the wall and inadvertently activate a secret panel within the mural. A passageway opens up at the north wall, exposing a set of stairs leading up to another level.

- ◆ If you choose to explore the secret passageway, turn to 197.

- ◆ If you would rather see where the doorway leads, turn to 64.

130

ENCOUNTER!

LIZARDMAN   SKILL: 2   DAMAGE: 3   HEALTH: 12

If you are victorious, turn to 178.

131

Your jaw nearly drops through the floor as you feast your eyes on more treasure than you have ever seen. Gold and silver trinkets and coins, jewels and a variety of artifacts fill the room. In the centre of the room resting on a pedestal is a glowing red jewel. You have discovered the **Ruby of Power**! You step through the piles of coins and jewels scattered on the floor and make your way towards the fabled jewel. As you attempt to pick it up, a door on the east side of the room opens up and standing before you is the dreaded Gore, Overlord of the Labyrinth of the Minotaur. He stands nearly ten-feet-tall, and has huge muscles that give him the appearance of being chiselled out of rock. The monster is wielding a glowing battle axe in both hands.

"Who dares enter my private chambers?" Gore bellows, as he points his magical battle axe in your direction.

You need to think fast!

- ◆ If you respond by attempting to break the ice with **Laughter**, turn to 228.

- ◆ If you retrieve your **Vial of Green Liquid** and throw it at the minotaur, turn to 265.

- ◆ If you pick up the **Ruby of Power** and throw it at the minotaur's feet, turn to 80.

- ◆ If you raise your weapon and prepare to defend yourself, turn to 136.

132

The hallway leading away from the kitchen has two wooden doors. One has a sign on it that reads: **PANTRY, KEEP OUT!** The other door has no sign. If you choose to explore the pantry, turn to 255. If you choose to open the other door, turn to 283.

133

You are given a horse and begin your trip to the Labyrinth of the Minotaur, escorted by two soldiers from the Royal Guard. The first guard is a stocky dwarf brandishing a battle axe, who is obviously annoyed that he was pulled away from his mead drinking to escort you on your journey. The second guard is a tall, grey-haired man covered in battle scars. He wields a bow, arrows and a short sword. A few hours into your ride, the guards stop so the dwarf can relieve himself by a tree.

What will you do?

- If you try to ride away and escape, turn to 12.

- If you attempt to sneak up on the dwarf and slap his buttocks while he relieves himself, turn to 291.

- If you attack the royal guardsman armed with the bow and arrow, turn to 60.

- If you wait for the dwarf to finish and continue on to the Labyrinth of the Minotaur, turn to 140.

134

As you move towards the next door a voice yells, "I wouldn't go in there if I were you! Those creatures will tear you to pieces."

You turn around and see the dwarf staring at you, gripping a forging hammer.

"Now then, what brings you to my forge?" he asks.

- ◆ If you claim to be a trader looking to barter, turn to 226.

- ◆ If you claim to be Gore's servant, there to pick up an item for your master, turn to 143.

135

You break out your juggling balls and begin tossing them in the air. The lizardman takes a swing with his war hammer and swats them far away. Remove them from your **Inventory**. You pull out your weapon and prepare to defend yourself. Turn to 130.

136

Gore laughs and raises his battle axe.

"Prepare to die, worm!" he yells as he charges towards you.

ENCOUNTER!

GORE   SKILL: 4   DAMAGE: 4   HEALTH: 15

If you are victorious, turn to 56.

137

You tiptoe up to the slumbering harpy.

- ◆ If you strike it with a **Silver Dagger**, turn to 248.

- ◆ If you hit it with a **Wooden Club**, turn to 104.

- ◆ If you whack it with a **Sack of Manure**, turn to 273.

- ◆ If you give it a swift kick from your boot, turn to 17.

138

The Bugglebees are happy to offer what they can to assist you on your quest. You may choose any one of the following items to place in your **Inventory**:

- ◆ **Mini Slingshot**
- ◆ **Tiny Spear**
- ◆ **Vial of Healing**

You thank the tiny creatures for their charity and continue on your way. Turn to 6.

139

Seriously? You had the option to open the lantern and let it free and you smash the lantern instead?! Good job, Fool. The combination of the impact and shattered glass causes the faerie to die a gruesome death. You will spend the rest of your days carrying around the Ruby of Power, wandering the labyrinth, lost forever inside the tunnels. If only you had found a magical creature that could help you escape... your quest has ended.

140

As you and your armed chaperones approach the entrance to the labyrinth, you are met by a small band of goblins.

"Hand over your horses, weapons and gold, or meet your demise!" one of the goblins screams as it approaches you brandishing a wooden club.

The royal guardsmen laugh at the small, green creature's bravado.

"Move aside, disgusting creatures, or I shall slay you where you stand," the dwarf replies.

The goblin raises his club and lets out a battle cry as he rushes towards the guard with the two remaining goblins following its lead.

◆ If you charge in and join the battle, turn to 30.

◆ If you choose to leave the guards to fend for themselves and head for the entrance to the labyrinth turn to 217.

◆ If you get between both parties and attempt to calm the situation using **Laughter**, turn to 163.

141

The eye of the cyclops opens wide as he sees you remove the **Harpy Egg** from your sack. He takes the egg from you and gently places it on his chopping block. He walks over to you and pats your head with his giant hand.

"Master be very pleased, him love harpy omelettes," the cyclops says. "Egg very hard to find. Plus, harpy scratch and bite. Me hate that."

The cyclops opens up a wooden chest and removes a large golden mallet.

"This help you get more eggs for me. You smash stupid harpy good!"

Add **The Nutcracker** to your **Inventory**.

- If you choose to offer the cyclops another item, return to 293.
- Otherwise, turn to 298.

142

Upon searching the ogre, you find a key with a minotaur's horns engraved on the handle. Add the **Gold Key** to your **Inventory**. You make your way through the doorway and continue exploring the palace. Turn to 35.

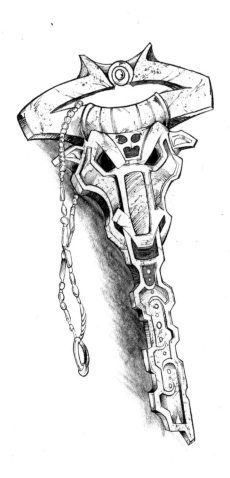

143

The dwarf nods and walks over to an armour rack and returns with a large iron bracer. Add the **Iron Bracer** to your **Inventory**.

"The Master will be pleased with my latest creation," the dwarf says. "Now deliver it with great haste! You know he hates to be kept waiting."

The dwarf ushers you out the northern door towards the minotaur's chambers. Turn to 64.

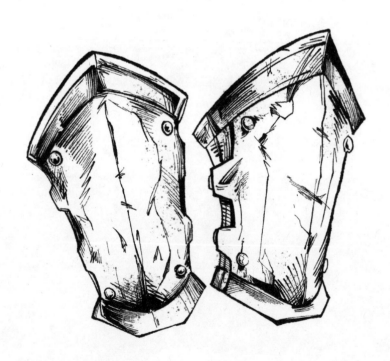

144

You rummage through your items to find something to break the ice.

- ◆ If you pull out an **Iron Spike** and **Wooden Club**, turn to 94.
- ◆ If you pull out a **Rusty Dagger**, turn to 162.
- ◆ If you pull out a **Vial of Green Liquid**, turn to 276.
- ◆ If you choose not to use these items, or do not have them, turn to 208.

145

The Queen calls for the Royal Guard standing outside the Princess' chambers.

"Kill this Fool!" she cries.

The guards unsheathe their weapons and attack. You're dead, Fool, and rightfully so. Mother-daughter combos are yucky. Go back to the start, Sir Creeps-A-Lot.

146

You are unable to find any keys. Annoyed, the witch curses you for your incompetence. Subtract -1 **Luck** from your score. You find a path leading out of the dungeon and follow it after offering the witch a few curse words of your own. Turn to 19.

147

Make a **Laughter** roll.

- If you succeed, turn to 154.
- If you fail, turn to 294.

148

Who are you kidding? You plant your foot into the door and are reminded of why you became a jester and not a warrior. Not only does the door not budge, but the impact also causes you to stumble backwards down the steps back into the dining room. Lose **1 Health.** You decide to leave the door alone and explore the doorway leading out of the dining room. Turn to 64.

149

Taking great offence at your comments, the centaur takes aim with his pitchfork and throws it at you. Attempt a **Luck** roll. If you succeed, turn to 18. If you fail, turn to 269.

150

A blast of hot air hits you in the face as you enter. A dwarf is hammering away at a sword on an anvil next to a forge that takes up most of the room. The blacksmith stops his work the moment he spots you.

"What do you think you're doing in here?" the dwarf asks, as he eyes you suspiciously.

- ◆ If you claim to be a trader looking to barter, turn to 226.

- ◆ If you claim to be a servant of Master Gore, there to pick up an item, turn to 143.

151

The lizardman's eyes bulge out in excitement from seeing the puppets. He claps as you make the puppets dance around the stone path. At the end of your performance, you make the puppets bow and put them away. The lizardman walks over to you and gives you a hearty slap on the back.

"Excellent, human! You may pass. Follow the path of **NENEN**. It shall keep you safe on your journey."

You thank the lizardman for his advice and continue down the path. Turn to 264.

152

You open the top of the lantern and the faerie flies out and transforms into a beautiful winged elven woman standing before you.

"Words cannot express my thanks for freeing me from Gore's prison. I am forever in your debt," she says. "I am Freya, Queen of Elves and Fairies in the Kingdom of Naturilia. Now that I am free of that cursed lantern, I can use my magic once again. How may I reward my brave rescuer?"

- ◆ If you ask to be teleported back to the palace of the Kingdom of Opulentos, turn to 118.

- ◆ If you ask to be transported back to the entrance of the labyrinth to meet the knights that escorted you, turn to 195.

153

The imp flies over to you and takes the **Harpy Egg**. He inspects it momentarily before tossing it at Cuddles, who eats it in one bite. Remove the egg from your **Inventory**.

"Now, what else have you brought to trade?" the imp asks.

- ◆ If you offer **Mouldy Cheese**, turn to 99.

- ◆ If you offer **Icy Heart**, turn to 86.

- ◆ If you use the **Wand of Meteor Showers** to crush the dragon and imp with massive space rocks, turn to 271.

- ◆ If you choose to offer them nothing else and instead request entrance into the palace, turn to 292.

154

The naga laughs in response to your compliment.

"Well spoken, Fool. Master Gore may have some use for you," she says. The naga plays a new melody on her harp, unlocking the minotaur's chambers.

You open the door and walk inside. Turn to 164.

155

You kneel down and extend your right hand to the bug crawling on your leg. It accepts your offer and climbs onto your palm. Upon further inspection, you realize the creature is actually a tiny man adorned in bugshell armour.

"Hello, little fellow," you say to the miniature man.

"Hail, giant! I am Thorax, captain of the guard. What brings you to the land of the Bugglebee people?"

"I am on a quest to retrieve the Ruby of Power, sent by King Opulentos. The King intends for me to meet my doom in this place, but I intend to overcome the odds and return with the artifact, so I may throw it at his majesty and knock his crown off of his fat head. And as he holds his skull and screams in pain, I shall slap the Queen on her bottom, then toss the Princess over my shoulder, bring her to my quarters and, if she's willing, make wild caveman love to her!"

The group of Bugglebees appear impressed with your answer.

"Your King has the soul of the most wretched of spiders!" Thorax shouts.

The horde of tiny men boo and hiss at the mention of spiders, obviously holding great disdain for the eight-legged insects. Turn to 88.

156

After being struck by the witch's spell, you immediately shrink down to the size of the bugglebees. You attempt to curse at the witch, but all that comes out is, "Ribbit!"

The witch you mocked has turned you into a frog. You will live the rest of your days chasing flies in the dungeon until your final croak. Your quest has ended.

157

You attempt to offer the **Vial of Green Liquid**. The orc, unimpressed with your bribe, raises his weapon and attacks. Turn to 223.

158

You place your hand in the bag and pull out a pile of horse manure. The Great Hall erupts with laughter. You can feel something else at the bottom of the sack. You guide your hand through the manure and pull out the foreign object. It is a small iron spike.

"Looks like the Gods have not smiled upon you, Fool!" Dolus Malus laughs, as he tosses a lantern at your feet.

He definitely hasn't forgotten about your prank. Add the **Sack of Manure**, **Lantern** and **Iron Spike** to **Inventory**. Turn to 260.

159

Deeply offended by your comment, the Twiggle attacks!

ENCOUNTER!

TWIGGLE   **SKILL: 3**   **DAMAGE: 2**   **HEALTH: 7**

If you are victorious, turn to 238.

160

Your body is cut clean in half from Gore's swing. You stay alive long enough to watch your torso hit the floor. Staring up at the ceiling, the last thing you see is Gore standing over your body laughing triumphantly. Your quest has ended.

161

You shift your body to the left-side tunnel and continue to pick up speed as you approach a light signalling the end of your ride. You fly out of the tunnel and land in a giant pile of hay. You roll out of the hay pile and brush yourself off shortly before an angry voice catches your attention.

"Hey you, stop messing with my piles!" yells an angry voice.

You turn your head towards the sound of the voice and see a male centaur holding a pitchfork. He is chained at the hoof to a large stone, obviously a prisoner of this place. Behind him is a stone path.

- ◆ If you offer to try to free him from his chains, turn to 198.

- ◆ If you try to use **Laughter** to break the tension, turn to 106.

- ◆ If you ignore him and continue past him on the stone path, turn to 168.

162

After a few strikes, the **Rusty Dagger's** blade snaps off of its hilt and falls to the ground. Remove the item from your **Inventory**. The crack in the block of ice has not changed.

◆ If you choose to try another item, go back to 144.

◆ Otherwise, continue down the icy corridor and turn to 208.

163

You dismount from your horse and run up between the two parties.

"Hold! Why fight when we can dance?" you say as you reach into your sack and pull out your trusty Marotte. You shake it while you dance and roll around on the ground. The guards and goblins stop in their tracks and offer puzzled looks to each other. Perform a **Laughter** roll.

- ◆ If you succeed, turn to 207.

- ◆ If you fail, you must battle the goblins. Learn some better dance moves and turn to 30.

164

The heavy door slams shut behind you after you enter the mino-taur's chambers. A large bed carved from stone fills a corner of the room. The heads of fallen creatures adorn the walls of this room. Weapons of fallen adversaries are displayed on racks. The smell of freshly brewed foul-smelling potions fills the air. Before you stands Gore, ruler of the Labyrinth of the Minotaur. He is wielding a magical battle axe that emits a red glow.

"Who dares disturb me?" the minotaur says, gripping his axe tightly, ready to cut you down where you stand.

- ◆ If you attempt to use **Laughter** to diffuse the situation, turn to 228.

- ◆ If you have the **Vial of Green Liquid** and wish to throw it at Gore, turn to 265.

- ◆ If you choose to draw your weapon and attack, turn to 136.

165

The creature tosses the gold pieces away and screeches at you. Remove them from your **Inventory**.

- ◆ If you prepare to defend yourself, turn to 108.

- ◆ If you offer the harpy a **Mouldy Onion**, turn to 81.

- ◆ If you offer the harpy some **Mouldy Cheese**, turn to 259.

166

You place your foot against the wall to get some extra leverage to yank the jewel out using brute force. Your hand slips; you stumble backwards onto the table and sit on a fork. Lose **1 Health**. Your high-pitched scream alerts an ogre in the next room, who enters the dining room but stops to stare in amazement that a fork could get lodged so deeply in one's buttock. The ogre appears unsure what to make of you, but is looming with a massive stone club and appears ready to crush you with it, if necessary.

- ◆ If you pull out the fork, raise your weapon and prepare to defend yourself, turn to 194.

- ◆ If you decide to use **Laughter** to diffuse the situation, turn to 243.

167

You search the pantry and find an **Elixir of Healing**. Add the potion to your **Inventory**. You then quietly exit the pantry. Turn to 32.

168

You walk along the stone path until your way is blocked by a large lizardman that stinks of putrid fish. He is staring at you suspiciously and is carrying a large war hammer.

"Sssssstate your businesssss, puny human," the lizard-man demands.

If you respond:

- ◆ "Hello there, my lizard friend. I am on a noble quest to obtain the Ruby of Power for King Opulentos. This quest is meant to end my life, but I will prove him wrong by obtaining the artifact, returning to the Kingdom, and sliding into bed with the lusty Princess." Turn to 295.

- ◆ "Quiet yourself, lizard lips, before I shove that war hammer up your scaly backside!" Turn to 211.

769

If your **Laughter** roll is successful, turn to 2. If you fail, turn to 54.

170

"How dare you!" the Princess says as she stomps on your twig and berries while calling for her guards.

Two members of the Royal Guard enter with Queen Opulentos to find you curled up in the fetal position trying to catch your breath.

"Mother, this Fool has deeply offended me and peeked at my sacred place. Take him to the Great Hall to be judged by Father!"

The Queen motions to the guards who grab you by your jingly bells and drag you out of the Princess' chambers. Turn to 100.

171

You place your hand on the mural and slide your palm across the painted wall. While inspecting the mural, you notice that one of the minotaur's eyes is a jewel that has been set into the wall.

- ◆ If you attempt to pry the jewel loose, turn to 45.

- ◆ If you choose to leave it alone and enter the doorway, turn to 64.

172

You scream for a few seconds until your fall ends with your body hitting a dirt floor with a hard thud. Unable to move your broken body, your final minutes are spent watching three hungry zombies make their way towards their next meal. Your quest has ended.

173

What item do you choose?

- ◆ If you choose your juggling balls, turn to 31.
- ◆ If you go for a **Vial of Green Liquid**, turn to 48.
- ◆ If you pull out a **Sapphire**, turn to 126.

174

You try the different keys on the ring until you find the correct one that unlocks the cell. The faint sound of someone snoring is coming from the chest.

- ◆ If you choose to investigate the chest, turn to 98.
- ◆ If you choose to leave the chest alone and make your way further into the labyrinth, turn to 212.

175

You find an **Iron Shield** in the pile of old gear that looks salvage-
able. Add it to your **Inventory**. As Cuddles the dragon enters the
courtyard, you duck behind the massive statue. The dragon sniffs
the air momentarily, before lying down and going to sleep. You
carefully tiptoe to the palace door and slip inside. Turn to 201.

176

After jumping through the portal, you collide with what smells like putrid fish and feels like a cavern wall. You fall to the ground and land on your duff. Lose **1 Health**. You look up and see a large lizardman staring down at you menacingly with a war hammer. The collision did not appear to have bothered him. You get back to your feet and brush yourself off.

"Ssssssssstate your bussssssssinesssssssss, puny human," the lizardman demands.

If you respond:

- ◆ "Hello there, my lizard friend. I am on a noble quest to obtain the Ruby of Power for King Opulentos. This quest is meant to end my life, but I will prove him wrong by obtaining the artifact, returning to the Kingdom, thrusting the ruby in between his buttocks, and sliding into bed with the lusty Princess." Turn to 295.

- ◆ "Quiet yourself, lizard lips, before I thrust that war hammer up your scaly backside!" Turn to 211.

177

You successfully sneak by the harpy and open the wooden chest. Turn to 73.

178

You search the lizardman's corpse and discover 10 gold pieces, a **War Hammer** and a **Potion of Healing**. Add them to your **Inventory**. After looting the body, you continue down the stone path. Turn to 264.

179

You are able to brace yourself and step away from the descending floor that you can now see descends into a dark pit. You decide to try your luck with the ladder and see where it goes. Turn to 287.

180

You place your feet firmly on the next panel and hold your breath in anticipation. Nothing happens. Where do you step next?

- ◆ If you step west, turn to 209.
- ◆ If you step east, turn to 282.
- ◆ If you step north, turn to 41.

181

Your feel a burning sensation from the lightning spark that strikes your back. Lose **2 Health**. You run towards a path leading out of the dungeon to avoid more zaps at the hands of the witch. Turn to 19.

182

After a few moments of awkward silence, you try to walk past the lizardman, but he blocks your path.

- If you attempt to use **Laughter** to break the ice, turn to 284.

- If you pull out a weapon and attack, turn to 130.

- If you explain your quest for The Ruby of Power and your need to continue down the path, turn 295.

183

The vampire falls to the ground from the impact of your last strike. His weapon flies out of his hand and he looks at you with fear in his eyes.

"Yield, vampire, or I shall destroy you," you warn the creature, while offering him a hand to help him up.

The vampire accepts his defeat, and you help him up to his feet.

"You bested me in combat and have allowed me to continue my undead existence. You have my respect and gratitude," the vampire says, and hands you his weapon and a potion as a gift. Add a **Bronze Sword** and an **Elixir of Health** to your **Inventory**.

You ask the vampire if you can travel through his lair to get deeper into the minotaur's labyrinth. He agrees and points you to a door on the opposite end of his lair. You thank him and continue on your quest. Turn to 244.

184

ENCOUNTER!

ZOMBIE 1   SKILL: 1   DAMAGE: 1   HEALTH: 8

ZOMBIE 2   SKILL: 1   DAMAGE: 1   HEALTH: 8

When you battle the zombies, the creatures are slow enough that you can battle them one at a time. After battling ZOMBIE 1, if you are victorious, go directly into battle with ZOMBIE 2. If you defeat them both, turn to 68.

185

You toss the **Water Flask** to the orc, who drinks from it and becomes enraged when realizing there is no ale inside. The orc throws the flask to the floor and smashes it with his sword. Remove it from your **Inventory**. The creature raises its weapon and attacks. Turn to 223.

186

The rocky corridor stops at an old wooden door. It is locked. You can hear something on the other side.

- ◆ If you knock on the door, turn to 15.
- ◆ If you have the **Rusty Key** and would like to try it in the door, turn to 230.

187

You pull the fork from your buttock and place it in your mouth as if tasting a fancy meal for the first time.

"Hmm, I'm afraid the rump isn't quite ready yet, my friend," you say to the ogre, who lets out a loud laugh in response.

He then rubs his eyes, sits down in the corner and falls asleep. As he begins to snore, one of his massive hands open up, and a key falls out of his palm onto the floor. You quietly move towards him and pick it up. Add the **Gold Key** to your **Inventory**. You tiptoe past the slumbering monster through the doorway and continue exploring the palace. Turn to 35.

188

A large orc walks into the dungeon and sees you standing by the cell that once held the witch. The orc screams a battle cry, pulls out its weapon and attacks.

ENCOUNTER!

ORC   SKILL: 2   DAMAGE: 3   HEALTH: 12

If you are victorious, turn to 289.

189

You raise your weapon and prepare for battle but are quickly overwhelmed by the sheer number of attackers. The creatures dismember you and spend the remainder of their training time playing hot potato with your decapitated head. Your quest has ended.

190

You drink the **Potion of Invisibility** and vanish before the creature's eyes. It stares at the spot where you still stand completely bewildered. Remembering you only have a short time before the potion loses its effects, you quickly tiptoe past the Icy Kell and continue down the path. Turn to 208.

191

While rummaging through the old gear for anything of value, the sound of weapons and armour clanging together attracts the attention of Cuddles the dragon. Before you have a chance to react, you are crushed under the weight of one of Cuddles' massive claws. Your quest has ended.

"Back, foul bugs!" You scream out as you kick your legs making the bugs fly in different directions. One of them cries out as it hits a cavern wall.

"Ouch! Watch where you're kicking, you giant buffoon!"

You stop kicking and kneel down to take a closer look at the bugs. Upon investigation, you realize that you haven't been stomping on bugs. You have been stomping on little people armed with miniature slings and pebbles wearing bugshell armour, and they're not happy about it. The little people begin pelting you in the face with pebbles. You stumble backwards and hit the back of your head on a rock, losing consciousness. Lose **1 Health** and turn to 202.

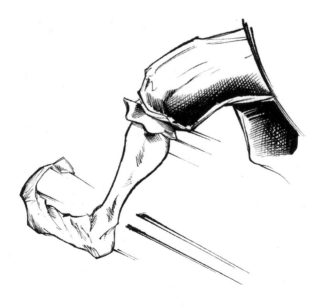

193

Thorax places his tiny spear into the lock attached to the chain around the centaur's leg. After a few pokes with his weapon, the lock opens.

"My thanks for the rescue! I am in your debt," the centaur says. "I shall help you escape this awful place."

Add **Gallup** to your **Allies** list. While accompanying you, Gallup offers **+2 Damage** in combat.

The three of you make your way down the stone path, further into the labyrinth. Turn to 168.

194

ENCOUNTER!

OGRE   SKILL: 2   DAMAGE: 4   HEALTH: 12

If you are victorious, turn to 142.

"Your wish is my command, my dear hero. Good luck in your travels," Queen Freya says before clapping her hands together, spraying your face with faerie dust.

You close your eyes and let out a loud sneeze. When you open your eyes, you realize that you are now standing at the entrance to the labyrinth. Laying against a tree fast asleep are the two members of the Royal Guard that escorted you on your quest. They appear to have decided to take a nap before heading back to the Kingdom. You kick the dwarf's boot, waking up both men. You smile and hold out the Ruby of Power. The guards jump to their feet, shocked that you have successfully completed your quest.

- ◆ If you deserted the guards and let them fight off the goblins without your help at the start of the quest, turn to 278.

- ◆ Otherwise, they celebrate your triumphant return and escort you back to the castle. Turn to 300.

196

You hold your breath, plug your nose and jump into the foul-smelling, rapidly moving water. The current carries you through a dark tunnel before spitting you out into a large pool of sewage. You gag while wading your way through the filth to a set of steps that take you onto land. The walls of this section of the labyrinth have been dug out to create prison cells that are built with iron bars and cell doors. You appear to have made your way into some sort of dungeon. A pile of bones from a variety of creatures fills up the south end of the room. Your scouting of the room is interrupted by a screeching voice.

"You! Come here and free me at once!" the voice commands.

You turn to see a woman with green skin covered in boils and sores standing behind the bars of one of the prison cells. Approaching her with caution, your eyes sweep the cell and notice that she has been shackled to the floor.

"Release me you foul-smelling wretch! The guard will be returning soon. Free me and you shall be rewarded," the woman says.

- ◆ If you have a **Tiny Spear** or Thorax and would like to attempt to pick the lock of the dungeon cell, turn to 121.

- ◆ If you search the dungeon for a key to the cell, turn to 146.

- ◆ If you respond, "Rot in your cell, you filthy hag! I have more pressing matters to attend to, like finding some soap to scrub my pantaloons!" Turn to 236.

197

You explore the secret chamber, which takes you up a set of stairs to a steel door.

- ◆ The door is locked. If you have a **Tiny Spear** or Thorax and would like to attempt to pick the lock, turn to 57.

- ◆ If you want to try to kick the door down, turn to 148.

- ◆ If you prefer to leave the door alone and try your luck with the doorway leading out of the dining room, turn to 64.

"Your offer is greatly appreciated, friend," the centaur says. "Gore has kept me imprisoned here for many years. If you can help me out of my bindings, I will help you escape. What brings you to such a wicked place?"

You explain that you were sent here by King and Queen Opulentos to retrieve the Ruby of Power and that it was a punishment meant to spell your doom for offences committed against the Royal Family. You add that you plan on succeeding in your mission and returning with the fabled jewel so you can place it in the hands of the King, then pull out your dirty bits and place those in the hands of the Princess, shortly before telling the Queen to get stuffed. The centaur laughs at your story.

"Well spoken, Fool. Now get me out of these chains so we may leave this hellish place," the centaur says.

You nod and search for an item in your inventory to free the centaur.

- ◆ If you retrieve Thorax and ask him to help, turn to 242.

- ◆ If you retrieve the **Tiny Spear**, turn to 256.

- ◆ If you choose to try the **Wooden Club** and **Iron Spike**, turn to 91.

- ◆ If you have none of these items, you must abandon the centaur and continue down the stone path. Turn to 168.

199

The lock will not open. You apologize to the witch and explain that you have no other means to release her. She casts a curse on you as punishment for your failure. Subtract -1 **Luck** from your score. You respond by shouting your own set of curse words before exiting the dungeon down a stone path. Turn to 19.

200

The guards shackle you and force you to kneel in front of the royal thrones while you await your fate. An hour later, King and Queen Opulentos enter the Great Hall alongside Dolus Malus, the court wizard, who you have always considered a pompous ass and all-around bad guy. The hall has filled with nobles and servants, many of whom you have often mocked, imitated and otherwise vexed.

"Rise, Fool!" the King commands.

As you stand, you notice Dolus Malus grinning and rubbing his hands together, practically brimming over with anticipation of something to come. Wizards doth sucketh the heftiest of donkey parts.

"Your unwillingness to comply with the Princess' request has greatly offended your Queen and King. For this, I should have you locked in the dungeon for the rest of your days," King Opulentos says. "However, after careful consult with the Queen and our loyal advisor, the wise Dolus Malus, we have decided to offer you an opportunity for absolution."

You nod, praying forgiveness will come in the form of anything other than a suicidal run through the Labyrinth of the Minotaur, one of the King's favourite ways to dispatch subjects he dislikes.

"Instead of heading to the castle dungeon, you shall make your way to the Labyrinth of the Minotaur and retrieve the ancient Ruby of Power," King Opulentos says, as laugher and dread fill the Great Hall. "Our bravest knights and adventurers seeking glory for the past two centuries have failed to retrieve the magical jewel, believed to rest in the lair of an ancient beast that resides within the labyrinth. Now you, Stultus Insanis Rusticus, shall go on this honoured and ancient quest to honour your King and Queen and bring great prestige to our kingdom."

You curse under your breath as you listen to the people in the court snicker and whisper to each other about your impending doom. Dolus Malus steps forward holding three small sacks.

"Noble Fool, your quest will be a perilous one," Malus says. "You will need to be well equipped if you are to survive your journey and bring back the fabled Ruby of Power. I have enchanted these sacks and filled them each with items that can assist you on your quest. You may choose only one for your journey, so choose wisely."

You're sure he's totally screwing with you – revenge for slipping a spike onto his seat during last year's royal banquet. Malus had to wear a pillow for a month, and you're certain he hasn't forgotten about it.

"Choose, Fool. Let fate guide your hand," he says with a mischievous grin.

Which one do you choose?

- ◆ If you choose the blue sack, turn to 158.

- ◆ If you decide on the purple sack, turn to 221.

- ◆ If you choose the green sack, turn to 240.

201

The inside of the palace is well lit from torches mounted onto the stone walls. The main entrance is surprisingly well decorated with a combination of paintings, vases, as well as silver and gold trinkets. If it wasn't for the damp, earthy walls and floor of the palace, you might think you are in the home of a noble or lord. The main entrance splits into two hallways.

- ◆ If you choose to go left, turn to 239.
- ◆ If you choose to go right, turn to 87.

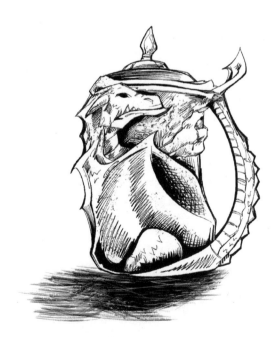

202

You awake to find yourself tied to the ground by hundreds of threads. One of the tiny men climbs onto your chest and begins to speak.

"How dare you squash us like insects under your boot! We are the Bugglebee people, and you have trespassed into our home and caused us great harm. Tell me one reason why I, Thorax, captain of the guards, should not sentence you to death by a thousand pebbles?

- ◆ If you apologize and beg forgiveness, turn to 11.

- ◆ If you try to use your strength to power your way out of the bindings, turn to 288.

- ◆ If you try to lighten the tension by telling a joke, turn to 111.

203

The harpy becomes enraged the moment you attempt to open the chest. Turn to 108.

204

"Ah! I see you are a practical collector. May the Elixir of Health bring you salvation during your darkest time," the vampire says.

Add the **Elixir of Health** to your **Inventory**. You thank him for the trade and ask if you may make your way through his den to continue on your quest. The vampire agrees and motions towards a door behind him. You leave his chambers and continue travelling further into the lair of the minotaur. Turn to 244.

205

The Queen calls for her Royal Guard. As they enter you attempt to raise your hands in surrender. Unfortunately, they were still under the Princess' purple satin sheet. You accidentally tear the sheet off the Princess, leaving her in the buff for everyone to admire. You and the guards stand hypnotized by her beautiful figure.

"Snap out of it, you fools," the Queen commands. "Take this disgusting wretch to the Great Hall for judgement!"

You can't divert your eyes from the Princess, continuing to stare and grin like the Fool you are as the guards drag you out of her chambers. Turn to 100.

206

You little sneaky-sneak! Make a **Luck** roll.

If you succeed, turn to 177.

If you fail, turn to 3.

207

The goblins burst into hysterical laughter at your silly dance. They join you in your antics and swing their clubs wildly in the air, shrieking with joy. The guards stare completely bewildered by your actions. At the end of the dance, the goblins jump and cheer. As you mount your horse, one of the goblins runs over and hands you a **Mouldy Onion** as payment for the entertainment. Add it to your **Inventory**. You thank the creature and continue towards the labyrinth. Turn to 245.

208

As you continue down the tunnel, the air warms and the icy path melts away, leading you into lush gardens. Flowers that have no business growing in these dark, damp caves are flourishing. Your path becomes illuminated by a combination of your lantern and dozens of firebugs flying in the air. You stop at an apple tree with red, luscious apples. Your stomach growls at the sight of the tasty fruit. A long, green snake slithers down the tree onto a branch close to you and begins to speak.

"To take one, you musssst leave ssssome," the snake hisses.

- ◆ If you take an apple and leave nothing, turn to 85.

- ◆ If you take an apple and leave **Magic Beans**, turn to 116.

- ◆ If you take an apple and leave a **Mouldy Onion**, turn to 218.

- ◆ If you ignore the apple tree and continue through the grove, turn to 14.

209

You move north but the next panel you step on collapses and you fall into a pit of darkness.

- ◆ Make a **Luck** roll. If you succeed, turn to 219.
- ◆ If you fail, turn to 172.

210

Princess Nerida giggles and calls you into her chambers. As you walk into her private bedroom, you are greeted by the Princess, who is dressed in a purple satin sheet tied together at the shoulder. Her long, raven-black hair flows down onto her ample bosom. Caught off guard by her untraditional garment and exposed skin, you ogle her before you can shift your eyes away.

"So, how do you intend to fill my bosom with laughter, my naughty jester?" she asks.

What will you do?

- ◆ If you juggle balls, turn to 36.
- ◆ If you perform a puppet show, turn to 66.
- ◆ If you dance, turn to 103.

211

Perform a **Laughter** roll.

- ◆ If you succeed, turn to 107.
- ◆ If you fail, turn to 20.

212

The path leading away from the dungeon smells of rotting meat and vegetables. The smell gets increasingly potent as you come to the end of the path. There is a ladder to your left. To your right is a dark corridor.

- ◆ If you choose to climb the ladder and see where it leads, turn to 287.
- ◆ If you choose to explore the corridor, turn to 237.

213

You grip the chain and give it a yank. The floor opens up underneath your feet and you are shot down a steep slide of smooth rock. You attempt to slow yourself down but the walls are too slick, preventing you from getting a proper grip. You can see a fork coming up that is lit by a torch. Above the right side are the words, "Choose Me." Above the left side are the words, "Go Away."

- ◆ If you choose to go right, turn to 78.

- ◆ If you choose to go left, turn to 161.

214

The Icy Kell smiles at you as you place the juggling balls into its right hand. Remove them from your **Inventory**. The creature opens up its left hand and forms a glowing icy sword. The weapon is made from the same magical ice as the frozen giant. Add the **Icebreaker** to your **Inventory**. You thank the creature and continue through the labyrinth. Turn to 208.

215

You push forwards with all of your might and break free from your bonds. This makes you sit up quickly, catapulting Thorax through the air like a mini projectile. He bounces off a cavern wall, and his broken body lands on the ground in front of the other Bugglebees. They recoil in horror and flee. You rise to your feet and continue exploring the tunnel. Turn to 6.

216

"How dare you insult my collectible tunic," the vampire says. "Prepare yourself for a duel!"

ENCOUNTER!

VAMPIRE   SKILL: 2   DAMAGE: 2   HEALTH: 12

If the creature's health falls below 5, you may choose to stop the battle.

- ◆ If you do, turn to 183.
- ◆ If you decide to fight to the death and win, turn to 253.

217

"Kiss my pantaloons!" you cry out as you ride towards the labyrinth, leaving the guards to fend for themselves. Turn to 245.

218

You place the **Mouldy Onion** in the soil by the tree. The ground opens up and swallows the rotten vegetable.

"A wisssse choice," the snake hisses before slithering away.

A branch of the tree extends towards you and offers you a ripe apple. You open your hand, and the fruit is placed in your palm. You happily eat the tasty fruit. Restore **3 Health.**

You place the apple core in the soil, turn to 250.

219

You scream as you plummet towards your doom. Closing your eyes, awaiting your final impact, you are happily surprised when you land on something squishy that collapses under your weight with a crunch-like sound. However, your joy quickly dissipates, as your nostrils are filled with the stench of squished zombie. You roll off the crushed corpse and begin to gag from the foul smell. Your retching is interrupted by the sounds of moaning coming from two dark corners of what appears to be some sort of sewer system. Rotted corpses and bones are scattered throughout the area. A fast-flowing stream of brown, foul-smelling water runs through the south side of the sewer. To the north is a path leading into another section of the labyrinth. While considering your next move, you notice the moaning becoming louder. You turn and see two zombies slowly making their way towards you.

- If you choose to battle the zombies, turn to 184.

- If you choose to run away down the path to the north, turn to 235.

- If you choose to jump into the water and see where the current takes you, turn to 196.

220

You search the orc and find 5 gold pieces, a **Bronze Sword**, a **Ring of Keys** and **Boar Meat**. Add these items to your **Inventory**. After collecting the spoils of battle, you continue down the path deeper into the labyrinth. Turn to 212.

221

As you slide your hand inside you feel a sharp, stabbing pain and drop the bag. Lose **1 Health**. The court erupts in laughter. While cursing under your breath, you carefully pick up the bottom of the sack and spill its contents to the floor. You retrieve a **Rusty Dagger**, a **Lantern** and a piece of **Mouldy Cheese**. Add these items to your **Inventory**. Turn to 260.

222

The cyclops is impressed with your offer and hands you a **Potion of Health**. Add the potion to your **Inventory**.

- ◆ If you choose to offer him another item, return to 293.

- ◆ Otherwise, turn to 298.

223

ENCOUNTER!

ORC   SKILL: 2   DAMAGE: 3   HEALTH: 12

If you are victorious, turn to 220.

224

You show the **Iron Bracer** to the naga, who nods in approval of your delivery. She plays a new melody on her harp, unlocking the minotaur's chambers.

You open the door and walk inside. Turn to 164.

225

As you step onto the panel you hear a clicking sound. Before you can respond, a spiked pole shoots out from a wall towards you. Make a **Luck** roll.

- ◆ If you succeed, turn to 7.
- ◆ If you fail, turn to 101.

226

You explain that you are a trader looking for new weapons and armour.

"I cannot trade any of these items without permission from Master Gore. You must take your request up with him," the dwarf says, motioning you to a door in the northern end of the room.

You nod and exit the forge through the north, leaving the dwarf to his tasks. Turn to 64.

227

You pick up the **Rusty Key** and continue moving deeper into the labyrinth. Add the key to your **Inventory**. Turn to 281.

228

"You know, I used to think I was the horniest bugger in all the land. But looking at you, I can see I no longer hold that title," you respond.

Gore charges you and swings his giant battle axe. Make a **Luck** roll.

- ◆ If you succeed, you dodge the attack and prepare to defend yourself. Turn to 136.

- ◆ If you fail, turn to 160.

229

What do you offer?

- ◆ If you offer the **Icy Heart**, turn to 29.

- ◆ If you offer the **Sapphire**, turn to 46.

- ◆ If you offer the **Sack of Manure**, turn to 95.

- ◆ If you have none of these items, return to 235.

The **Rusty Key** fits perfectly into the door. You slowly open the door and peek inside. You see a harpy asleep in its nest. Next to the nest is a small wooden chest.

- ◆ If you choose to close the door, and go back to try the other path, turn to 241.

- ◆ If you decide to attack the sleeping harpy, turn to 137.

- ◆ If you attempt to sneak into the harpy's lair and open up the wooden chest, turn to 206.

231

You pull out your jester's staff and proceed to dance and sing a tune you think will amuse the imp.

> *An imp is a pest with tiny wings,*
> *Takes all the stuff that you can brings.*
> *If you're not careful, you soon will be broke,*
> *So pull out your sword, and give 'em a poke!*

The imp is unimpressed by your song. He flutters over to a skull impaled on a pole at the top of the steps. The imp yanks on the skull, opening its mouth, causing the steps under your feet to give way and turn into a steep, slippery ramp. You fall on your backside and begin to slide down away from the palace. A dark hole now lies where the bottom step once was. Unable to stop, you are cast into the darkness. Turn to 267.

232

Insulted, the cyclops attacks!

ENCOUNTER!

CYCLOPS   SKILL: 3   DAMAGE: 4   HEALTH: 13

If you survive, turn to 53.

233

As you walk forwards, you can feel something crawling up your leg. You lower your lantern and see what appears to be a bug with a brown shell inching towards your knee. There appears to be dozens more around you. Many of them are climbing onto your boots.

- ◆ If you kick the bug off your leg and frantically start stomping on the bugs, turn to 192.

- ◆ If you crouch down and offer your hand to the bug to inspect it further, turn to 155.

234

The creature's skin cracks all over upon your final strike. It falls dead at your feet and shatters into a thousand pieces on impact with the cavern floor. Upon searching the creature, you find its frozen heart. Add the **Icy Heart** to your **Inventory**. You continue further down the icy path, deeper into the cavern. Turn to 208.

235

You can feel the heavy moisture in the air and under your boots as the dirt path turns to mud. Your boots begin to stick to the cavern floor as you make your way towards an iron door. A slot opens up on the upper section of the door and a pair of bright red eyes meet your gaze.

"Turn back, mortal. Unless you wish this place to be your tomb," a voice warns.

How do you respond?

- ◆ If you decide to turn back and try your luck travelling down the stream, turn to 196.

- ◆ If you choose to offer a gift to the mysterious creature, turn to 229.

- ◆ If you respond, "Open this door at once! I am on a noble quest and will not be impeded by a pair of floating eyeballs," turn to 286.

236

As you start to leave the dungeon, the witch chants in an unknown language and strikes you in the back with a magic spell. Roll a die.

- If you roll 1 or 2, turn to 10.
- If you roll 3 or 4, turn to 181.
- If you roll 5, turn to 122.
- If you roll 6, turn to 156.

237

You walk a few steps into the corridor and begin to lose your footing. The floor is slippery due to it being covered in rotting food. You must make a **Luck** roll.

- If you succeed, turn to 179.
- If you fail, turn to 268.

238

The Twiggle dries up and crumbles into dust, becoming one with the soil at your feet. You continue to make your way through the grove. Turn to 14.

239

As you walk down the hall, the scent of something sweet fills your nostrils. You come to a wooden door with a sign that reads, "KITCHEN, KEEP OUT!" What do you do?

- ◆ If you kick the door open and yell, "What's cookin', good lookin'?" turn to 246.

- ◆ If you slowly open the door and peek inside, turn to 124.

240

You slip your hand in the sack and retrieve three **Magic Beans**, a **Lantern**, and a **Water Flask**. Court Wizard Dolus Malus looks disappointed at your choice. Breathing a sigh of relief, you pick up the items and add them to your **Inventory**. Turn to 260.

241

The deeper you move into the tunnel, the louder the sounds become. You hear what sounds like the pitter-patter of many tiny feet.

- ◆ If you continue to explore the tunnel, turn to 233.
- ◆ If you decide to go back and take the other path, turn to 186.

242

"Of course, my friend. I shall free this poor soul," Thorax says as he climbs down from your shoulder and walks over to the centaur. Make a **Luck** roll.

- ◆ If you succeed, turn to 193.
- ◆ If you fail, turn to 113.

243

If your **Laughter** roll succeeds, turn to 187. If you fail, turn to 79.

244

The path out of the vampire's lair has many twists and turns before ending at a ladder which leads to a wooden hatch in the ceiling. You climb the ladder, open the hatch and cautiously pop your head inside. Spotting no movement, you climb inside the room. The scent of molten metal is in the air. The small room is warm and dry. A pile of iron ore takes up a corner of the room, while shelves of smithing tools and iron ingots fill up the remaining space. There is a wooden door leading out of the storage room. You open the door and investigate your location further. Turn to 119.

245

A moss-covered cavern comes into view as you make your way to the entrance of the labyrinth. You dismount your horse and walk towards the entrance. All you know about this place is that it is a set of interconnected caves that many adventurers and scholars have lost their lives exploring. At your favourite pub, drunken men who claimed to be survivors of the labyrinth spoke of it housing all sorts of dangerous and magical creatures, although you were pretty sure most of them were spinning deceitful tales. After all, how can someone have the skills to survive the Labyrinth of the Minotaur but not have the dexterity to pass water into a bucket? It just doesn't add up. You take a deep breath, light your lantern and step into the dark entrance. Turn to 34.

246

You kick open the door and yell, "What's cookin', good lookin'?" You startle a large, muscular cyclops wearing a chef's hat and apron, who stumbles and drops a tray of desserts on the floor. The cyclops gives you an angry look before picking up a massive meat cleaver and advancing towards you screaming, "You ruin Master's cupcakes!"

ENCOUNTER!

CYCLOPS   SKILL: 3   DAMAGE: 4   HEALTH: 13

If you survive, turn to 53.

247

You grab the skull of the deceased, pop the head off and slip your hand inside it so you can manipulate its bony jaw.

"Hello, Mr. Bones. 'Tis a fine day, is it not?" you say to the skull.

"Why yes it is, noble and great jester of the Royal Court," you make the skull reply, moving its mouth open and closed.

"You're too kind, Mr. Bones. I hate to be a bother, but would you mind if I borrowed your key? It looks like it could be helpful on my quest. You see, I was sent on a quest by King Opulentos. He wishes for me to locate the fabled Ruby of Power. The quest was meant to spell my doom. But my hope is to defy these perilous odds, so I may return to the Kingdom with the ruby in hand so I may shove said fabled jewel between his regal buttocks as he slumbers then ravish his daughter, the Princess."

As you begin to make the skull speak again, the skeleton's bony hand opens up and offers you the key. You place the skull back on the body of the skeleton and pick up the **Rusty Key** and add it to **Inventory**.

"My thanks to you, Mr. Bones! May you rest peacefully for all eternity," you say as you continue further into the labyrinth. Turn to 281.

248

You sneak up to the slumbering harpy and plunge your weapon into its back. The creature jumps to its feet screeching in pain. It has been injured but has become enraged from your attack.

ENCOUNTER!

HARPY   SKILL: 2   DAMAGE: 2   HEALTH: 7

If you are victorious, turn to 51.

249

ENCOUNTER!

ICY KELL   SKILL: 2   DAMAGE: 3   HEALTH: 12

The creature's hard skin offers additional protection from attacks from standard weapons. It receives -1 Damage from every strike. If you have a weapon that does 2 or more Damage, you may continue to battle the creature.

- ◆ If you would prefer to try to use an item, turn to 173.

- ◆ If you defeat the creature in battle, turn to 234.

250

The tree extends another branch to you and places a second apple in your hand. You add the **Red Apple** to your **Inventory** and continue to make your way through the grove. Turn to 14.

251

The dungeon is filled with a variety of torture devices, none of which will be helpful to take with you on your quest. You spot a treasure chest inside a locked cell in a corner of the dungeon.

- ◆ If you would like to try to unlock the cell using the **Ring of Keys**, turn to 174.

- ◆ If you choose to ignore the chest and leave the dungeon to continue exploring the labyrinth, turn to 212.

252

With the minotaur overlord Gore defeated, you decide to help yourself to his loot. The **Ruby of Power** shines brightly on a pedestal in the middle of the room. You carefully pick it up and place it in your sack. Add it to your **Inventory**. In addition to hordes of gold coins and jeweled trinkets, you discover a magic lantern emitting a warm, blue glow. You pick it up and look inside. To your surprise, you find a faerie that appears to be trapped inside.

- ◆ If you open the lantern and set the faerie free, turn to 152.

- ◆ If you decide to be a jerk and shake the lantern vigorously to see what will happen, turn to 263.

- ◆ If you choose to be an even bigger jerk and smash the lantern on the ground to set the faerie free, turn to 139.

253

The vampire turns into dust and leaves behind a **Bronze Sword**. Add the weapon to your **Inventory**. Looking around its lair, you see dozens of strange items on shelves, barrels and tables. It's impossible to identify any of the items. You make your way through the vampire's lair and exit out a door that brings you deeper into the labyrinth of the minotaur. Turn to 244.

254

Deeply offended by your rejection, the harpy rises to its feet and attacks. Turn to 108.

255

The pantry door is locked. Unable to open it, you decide to enter the other door, turn to 283.

256

The centaur presents its chained leg to you as you carefully manoeuvre the **Tiny Spear** in the lock. He appears anxious, so you attempt to use **Laughter** to calm him down.

- ◆ If you succeed, turn to 112.
- ◆ If you fail, turn to 277.

257

The naga nods and goes back to concentrating on playing her music. You place the **Gold Key** in the lock. Success! You unlock the door and enter the minotaur's quarters. Turn to 164.

258

The cyclops sniffs the cheese and nods his head, approving of the ingredient. He hands you 10 gold pieces. Remove the **Mouldy Cheese** from **Inventory**.

- If you choose to offer him another item, return to 293.

- Otherwise, turn to 298.

259

The harpy is repulsed at the sight and smell of the **Mouldy Cheese**. It backs away from you and returns to its nest, and motions for you to leave her lair through a trap door next to her nest.

- If you walk towards the trap door, turn to 23.

- If you attempt to open the small wooden chest, turn to 203.

260

You collect your quest items and thank Dolus Malus for his assistance, secretly hoping that one day you'll be able to return the favour to the puffed-up spellcaster.

"It is time for you to begin your quest," King Opulentos commands. "My Royal Guards will accompany you to the Labyrinth of the Minotaur to ensure your safe transport. Now go, Fool. Go and make your King and country proud!"

Turn to 133.

261

While rummaging through the pile of gear, most likely from fallen adventurers, you hear the booming sound of dragon feet coming towards you. Make a **Luck** roll.

- ◆ If you succeed, turn to 175.
- ◆ If you fail, turn to 191.

262

You walk over and sit in the harpy's nest, surprised to find it extremely comfortable. The smelly creature then throws you on your back and pulls off your pantaloons with her talons. If you were a scholar of magical creatures, you would have known that flinging feces at a harpy throws them into a lust-filled frenzy. Aroused and nervous, you watch as the monster mounts you and starts to make sweet, sweet harpy love to you, which you decide isn't so bad. After you receive ninety seconds of bliss, the harpy kisses your forehead and passes out in her nest. You quietly place what's left of your pantaloons back on and slip out of the nest. On your way out of the nest you notice a **Harpy Egg**, which you pick up and place in your **Inventory**. Next, you turn to the wooden chest.

- ◆ If you choose to search the wooden chest, turn to 73.

- ◆ If not, you open up the trap door and descend further into the labyrinth, turn to 9.

263

You big jerk! Shaking the lantern causes the faerie to bounce off the walls of the lantern. The magical creature lays dead inside its prison. You will spend the rest of your days wandering though the labyrinth with the Ruby of Power, never finding a way out. Your quest has ended.

264

The stone path begins to narrow as you venture forth. A foul smell fills your nostrils. The stench gets worse as you come to a room at the end of the corridor. As soon as you step inside, the path behind you becomes blocked by falling rocks. The square room you entered is lit by torches hanging from the cavern walls. Square-shaped panels cover the floor in a 3 x 3 formation. A sign on the wall with the words, "WATCH YOUR STEP!" inscribed on it hangs next to the entrance. With no choice but to continue moving forwards, you must choose a path. You step on the square directly north of you. Nothing happens. Where do you step from here?

♦ If you decide to step north, turn to 209.

♦ If you decide to step east, turn to 297.

265

You throw the **Vial of Green Liquid** at Gore, who blocks the attack with his magical battle axe. Remove the item from your **Inventory**. The acid in the vial burns his hands, causing him to drop the weapon on the ground. The minotaur roars at you and charges you with its horns. You raise your weapon and prepare for the final battle! Turn to 26.

266

As you fly towards the massive stalagmites, you close your eyes and curse King and Queen Opulentos for sending you to a painful and pointy doom. Your quest has ended.

267

While freefalling deeper into the darkness, you shut your eyes and pray for some sort of miracle to save you. Make a **Luck** roll.

- ◆ If you succeed, turn to 219.

- ◆ If you fail, turn to 172.

268

You fall to the ground and slide down a foul-smelling ramp into a dark pit. Your body lands in a huge pile of rotting food. Before you are able to get to your feet, you feel something bite your leg. You light your lantern and realize you are surrounded by dozens of hungry gremlins. Upon smelling you, the creatures go into a feeding frenzy, and you suffer the death of a thousand nibbles. Your quest has ended.

269

The centaur's pitchfork strikes you in the leg, causing you to scream in agony. Lose **3 Health**. You pull the pitchfork out of your leg and wrap the wound. To spite the centaur, you decide to take his tool with you. Add the **Centaur's Pitchfork** to your **Inventory**. You hobble away from the centaur and continue down the stone path. Turn to 168.

270

As you turn your back and start to run, you feel the harpy's sharp talons dig into your shoulders. You start to scream, but your voice is silenced by the bird-like creature's beak piercing into your neck. You fall to your knees and begin to bleed out as the harpy feeds on your flesh. Your quest has ended.

271

Seriously? I just made that up! Now go back and offer something you actually have in your **Inventory**. No more cheating! Return to 5.

272

You creep slowly towards the ogre and place your hand on the key, slowly removing it from the monster's belt. Make a **Luck** roll.

- ♦ If you succeed, place the **Gold Key** in your **Inventory** and make your way up the stairs. Turn to 89.

- ♦ If you fail, the ogre awakens, and you must battle it. Turn to 47.

273

You open up the **Sack of Manure** and toss it onto the sleepy harpy. Remove it from your **Inventory**. The creature awakens and jumps to its feet. It is about to attack you with its talons when the harpy realizes that you have covered it in excrement. The bird-like creature lowers its talons and smiles at you with its many sharp, pointy teeth. It then lays back down in its nest, exposing its feathered breasts, and motions for you to join her.

◆ If you accept her invitation, turn to 262.

◆ If you refuse, turn to 254.

274

You jump on the centaur's back and yell, "To the Ruby of Power, noble steed!"

"Get off me, Fool, are you mad!?" the centaur yells as it bucks you off into the pile of hay.

The centaur points its pitchfork towards you and takes aim. As the creature is about to deliver a killing blow, it looks down at your garments and quickly calms down.

"Oh, you really are a Fool," he says while lowering his pitchfork. "Begone, before I change my mind and run you through!"

You nod and quickly scurry away from the centaur, making your way down the stone path. Turn to 168.

275

The door emits a loud creaking sound as it opens, alerting the creatures inside to your presence. Two orcs, three goblins and a lizardman all turn towards you brandishing their weapons. You appear to have stumbled into a training room. The creatures prepare to attack.

- ◆ If you raise your weapon and try to take on all of the creatures, turn to 189.

- ◆ If you attempt to use **Laughter** to calm the situation, turn to 169.

276

You open up the **Vial of Green Liquid** and recoil from the acidic, rancid aroma. Carefully, you pour the liquid into the crack in the ice. Remove it from your **Inventory**. The liquid eats through the ice and makes its way towards the creature inside. The ice block cracks in multiple places then explodes, sending icy projectiles in every direction. Make a **Luck** roll.

- ◆ If you roll a 1 or 2, turn to 43.

- ◆ If you roll a 3 or 4, turn to 71.

- ◆ If you roll a 5 or 6, turn to 280.

277

You slip and accidentally stab the centaur's leg. The centaur screams in pain then winds up and kicks you with enough force to toss you back into a hay pile. Lose **3 Health**. The centaur then tramples your **Tiny Spear**. Remove it from your **Inventory**. After catching your breath, you decide it would be best to leave the centaur alone and continue down the stone path. Turn to 168.

278

Remembering your disloyalty and cowardice, the dwarf guard headbutts you in your royal jewels and takes the Ruby of Power. You collapse to the ground grasping your twig and berries.

"Thanks, Fool. Now we shall be the heroes!" the dwarf yells as the two guards jump onto their steeds and gallop away.

You have lived to tell the tale of how you survived the labyrinth, slayed the dreaded Gore and retrieved the Ruby of Power! Of course, with the guards returning to the King and taking all the credit it's unlikely anyone will ever believe you. But hey, you're alive, right? So, huzzah! Sort of...

279

Offended by your refusal to hand over the juggling balls, the Icy Kell attacks, turn to 249.

280

You close your eyes and cover your head. After a few moments you hear a loud thump. You open your eyes and realize you are completely unharmed. The Gods have smiled upon you. Add +1 **Luck** to your score. You brush a few tiny pieces of ice from your body and stare at what looks like some sort of ice giant lying dead at your feet. As you approach the body, it shatters into tiny pieces. While searching the remains you discover an **Icy Heart**, which you add to your **Inventory**. You then continue down the icy corridor in search of the Ruby of Power. Turn to 208.

281

A fork appears in the cavern, offering two paths. On the left, you believe you hear faint movements. On the right, there is nothing but silence.

- ◆ If you choose to go left, turn to 241.
- ◆ If you choose to go right, turn to 186.

282

You step onto the panel without incident, breathing a sigh of relief. Where do you step next?

- ◆ If you step north, turn to 65.

- ◆ If you step west, turn to 180.

283

You open the wooden door and peer inside. The hallway leads into a dining room area. A large stone table and chairs take up most of the space in the room. A large mural depicting a battle between the minotaur and his horde and an army of elves and fairies has been painted on the walls of the room. There is a doorway leading out of the dining area.

- ◆ If you choose to inspect the mural in detail, turn to 171.

- ◆ If you choose to leave the dining area and continue your way through the palace, turn to 64.

284

What **Laughter** tool do you use?

- ◆ If you use juggling balls, turn to 135.
- ◆ If you use puppets, turn to 151.

285

The lock on the cell door opens.

"Good work. Now free me from this shackle!" the witch commands.

You must make another **Luck** roll.

- ◆ If you are successful, turn to 37.
- ◆ If you fail, turn to 110.

286

"Then perhaps you need to see the rest of me, foolish mortal," the creature says as it opens the door.

Standing before you is a vampire with a large belly that nearly protrudes out of his green tunic, which has the words "DUNGEON CON" inscribed on the chest.

"Quake in terror from my undead aura! Run in horror before I feed upon you and turn you into my undead minion," he says.

If you reply:

- ◆ "What kind of living does an undead jester make these days? Would I get dental?" turn to 76.

- ◆ "If I soil my pantaloons it shall not be from fear, but from laughter at your ridiculous clothing. Nice dress, my lady!" turn to 216.

287

The ladder leads to a trap door. You open it and climb inside what appears to be a pantry. Shelves of pickled foods and sacks of various ingredients fill the room. You place your ear to the door leading out of the room. You don't hear anything, so it is probably safe to slip out undetected.

- ◆ If you leave the room immediately, turn to 32.
- ◆ If you stay and search the pantry, turn to 167.

288

You attempt to break the bindings with raw force.

- ◆ If you roll a 1, 2, 3 or 4, turn to 44.
- ◆ If you roll a 5 or 6, turn to 215.

289

You search the orc and find 5 gold pieces, a **Bronze Sword**, a **Ring of Keys** and **Boar Meat**. Add these items to your **Inventory**.

◆ If you choose to search the dungeon, turn to 251.

◆ If you prefer to follow the path where the guard entered the dungeon, turn to 212.

290

As you juggle the balls, Cuddles becomes excited and decides to try to snatch one from the air, accidentally biting you in half. Bad dragon! Your quest has ended.

291

You place your pointer finger on your mouth signalling the archer to be silent as you sneak up behind the dwarf and slap him on his bare bottom. The startled dwarf stumbles accidentally, sprinkling yellow on his boots, causing the other guard to burst out laughing. The dwarf curses you and threatens to cleave you in two with his axe, so you quickly get back on your horse. The archer, impressed with your antics, hands you a **Silver Dagger** to aid you on your quest. He says it will be especially useful in any encounters involving the undead. The dwarf continues to curse at you as he mounts his steed and you continue on your quest. Turn to 140.

292

"Well then, I thank you for the visit," the imp says as it flutters over to a skull impaled on a pole at the top of the steps. The imp yanks on the skull, opening its mouth, causing the steps under your feet to give way and turn into a steep, slippery ramp. You fall on your backside and begin to slide down away from the palace. A dark hole now lies where the bottom step once was. Unable to stop, you are cast into the darkness. Turn to 267.

293

The cyclops smiles a rotted, toothy grin.

"Oh boy, new ingredients! Me trade! Make new food, make master happy!" he says. "What you bring?"

If you offer:

- ◆ **Mouldy Cheese**, turn to 258.

- ◆ **Boar Meat**, turn to 90.

- ◆ **Harpy Egg**, turn to 141.

- ◆ **Beaker of Octopus Ink**, turn to 222.

- ◆ **Mouldy Onion**, turn to 39.

- ◆ **Magic Beans**, turn to 97.

- ◆ If you choose to trade no more items, turn to 298.

294

The naga hisses at you and equips all four of her arms with weapons. You prepare to defend yourself as she slithers towards you.

ENCOUNTER!

NAGA　　　SKILL: 2　　DAMAGE: 4　　HEALTH: 10

If you are victorious and have the **Gold Key**, you unlock the steel door and proceed into the minotaur's chambers. Turn to 164. If you do not have the **Gold Key**, you now have no means to gain entry into the minotaur's chambers. Your quest has ended.

295

Upon hearing of your quest to obtain the Ruby of Power, the lizardman raises his weapon and attacks!

ENCOUNTER!

LIZARDMAN　SKILL: 2　　DAMAGE: 3　　HEALTH: 12

If you are victorious, turn to 178.

296

What item do you offer?

- ◆ If you offer a **Water Flask**, turn to 185.

- ◆ If you offer a **Bag of Orc Teeth**, turn to 50.

- ◆ If you offer all of your gold pieces, turn to 24.

- ◆ If you offer a **Vial of Green Liquid**, turn to 157.

297

You hold your breath and step onto the next panel. Nothing happens. Now where do you go?

- ◆ If you step north, turn to 180.

- ◆ If you step east, turn to 225.

298

The cyclops thanks you for offering your ingredients. You ask him where you can find his master. Assuming you are looking to conduct further trades, the cyclops motions to a wooden door in the back of the kitchen. You thank him and continue to make your way through the palace. Turn to 132.

299

Thorax agrees to your request and decides to join you as your travelling companion. Add **Thorax** to your **Allies** list. While accompanying you, Thorax causes all creatures to take lose **1 Health** before the start of combat and offers you +1 **Luck** during your journey. You thank all of the Bugglebees and continue on your journey. Turn to 6.

300

As you march triumphantly through the castle grounds, you are met with confused looks from the Royal Staff who were sure they saw the King send you to your doom in a quest for the glory of the kingdom. You stroll through the door to the palace throne room and greet King and Queen Opulentos and Princess Nerida, who all look very surprised to see you.

Dolus Malus, the court wizard, raises his hand and is about to speak when you retrieve the Ruby of Power from your sack, rendering him speechless.

"Give this a polish, lad," you say as you toss the fabled jewel to the court mage, who fails to catch it, takes the massive stone off the chin and falls to the ground.

"I don't believe it. Is that truly the Ruby of Power?" King Opulentos asks.

You simply smile a toothy grin before snatching his crown off his head and placing it on your own, pinching the Queen's bottom and planting a firm kiss on the lips of the Princess.

"Your Fool has returned!" you yell triumphantly.

The King and Queen burst out in laughter and decide to throw a feast in your honour. That night your glorious return is celebrated twice. Once by the King, the Queen and all the Kingdom, and again later that night in the chambers of the ravishing Princess Nerida. HUZZAH!!

The End

ACKNOWLEDGEMENTS

Ever since I was a young lad, I have been drawn to fantasy books. If a book had club-wielding ogres, fire-breathing dragons, skilled archers, and sneaky rogues, it always caught my attention. The first of these books to grab my attention were the dice-rolling, monster battling adventures created by Ian Livingstone and Steve Jackson (Fighting Fantasy – check them out, they're still amazing). I can honestly say that their books were the first that made me develop a passion for reading. While this silly adventure is unlikely to have the same effect, since it is not appropriate for that age range, I do hope that people from my generation who found a similar joy in reading these types of books will have a good laugh as they decide their fate in *Dungeon Jest: The Ruby of Power.*

This book was written during the early days of the COVID-19 coronavirus pandemic. Thanks to a toddler named Sebastian, who enjoyed waking up in the early morning hours for most of 2020, I had plenty of opportunities to cuddle with him on the couch and write this book via notepad and pen while he watched his cartoons and ate Eggo waffles. It was a fun experience putting this kind of book together. Between the regular editing procedures and trying to ensure all the paragraphs match up, it has certainly been a labour of love.

Thanks to my always amazing wife, Cristine, who has spent a great deal of the pandemic chasing after our three little ones, which has allowed me to put this book together while focusing on running my business (she even helped me lay out all the paragraphs for this book across the floor and checked them with me to ensure they were properly connected).

Regarding putting the book together, it wouldn't have been near as much fun to create without the awesome artistic skills of the curmudgeonly-but-lovable Jeff Fowler, whose mad sketching skills combined with the awesome inking of Corey King has resulted in all the incredible artwork. Thanks so much for your efforts in putting this together. The book will undoubtedly offer a far better reading experience due to your hard work!

Special thanks also go out to my supercool eagle-eyed editors, Nicole North and Rosanne Lake, for their great job finding my mistakes and for having the patience to connect each of the 300 paragraphs to ensure they follow the appropriate paths.

I hope my fellow bookworms enjoy this silly read and that it brings you many snorts and giggles during this strange time we live in.

Take care, stay safe and happy reading and writing!

ABOUT THE AUTHOR

 Andrew Snook has been working as a professional writer for more than a decade, first as a newspaper reporter in the Ottawa area and later as a magazine editor and feature writer for a variety of business publications and now as the owner of Snookbooks Publishing. His fiction and business writing have both won him international awards, which is neat, but he's happier knowing his fiction made someone laugh out loud at an inappropriate moment. In addition to Dungeon Jest: Ruby of Power, Snook is the author of The Remy Delemme Series and children's book series, The Snookie-Cookie Sisters, which is scheduled for release in mid-2022. He lives in Mississauga, Ontario, with his super-amazing wife, Cristine, his three awesomesauce kiddos Emily, Sofia and Sebastian, his curmudgeonly old dog, Merlin, his troublemaking puppy, Luna, Nibbler the hamster and Blueberry the betta fish.

ABOUT THE ARTIST

On a warm summer's eve in August 1977, a small crack of thunder (okay, more of a whimper, really) heralded the arrival of Jeffery Scott Fowler into this world.

Since he could hold a crayon, Jeff found a way to make his mark on every scrap of paper, napkin or wall he could find. A child of the 80's, his young mind soaked in a sugary-coated tsunami of comic books and Saturday morning cartoons.

Although his love for drawing never truly faded, Jeff made the decision to pursue a career in the stable world of film and television (insert sarcasm here). By trade, he's a video editor and director. Still steeped in the world of sci-fi, fantasy and superheroes, Jeff continues to not only illustrate, but also sculpts masks and cowls for people around the globe.

Jeff currently resides in Hamilton "The Hammer" Ontario with his wife, Diana, and their faithful canine companion, Remy.

More fun adventures from Andrew Snook

REMY'S DILEMMA

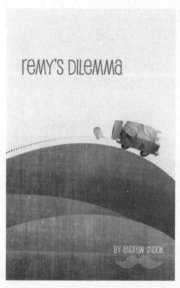

The world is coming to an end. That's what Remy Delemme believes, anyways. While double-checking his lifelong to-do list to ensure he has led a rich life, he realizes he hasn't come close to completing his goals. Panicked and short on time, Remy embarks on a chaotic road trip to complete the most important item on his bucket list – finding the answer to man's greatest question. There's just one problem. Detective Tobias Gray, the most respected criminal profiler in the Toronto Police Department, thinks Remy is a serial killer; and he's not the only one who has come to that conclusion. Armed with a green crayon, smiley-faced stamp and a pack of cigarettes in a race against time, the story's main character, Remy, carves a path of hilarious destruction, baffling and infuriating the police, his government and every other person he encounters.

Follow my adventures at www.snookbooks.com

REMY'S DILEMMA: SPECIAL DELIVERY

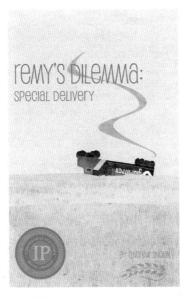

In Book II of the Remy Delemme Series, Remy finds himself detained in Prince Albert, Saskatchewan, arrested for crimes against the Glamerican government. To earn his freedom and avoid incarceration, a confused yet cooperative Remy is forced to work as a shadow agent for the government. Unfortunately for them, Remy isn't the criminal genius they pegged him for (nor is he even a regular kind of genius), and he inadvertently sets off a series of events that could spell doom for the entire world. Meanwhile, Toronto police detective Tobias Gray attempts to track him down and rescue Rose Maheen, the love of Remy's life who has mysteriously gone missing. Along with a cast of wickedly funny characters, including a grizzly moose addicted to maple beans and a retired curler turned philosophical hobo, the bumbling but ever-endearing Remy sets off across Western Canada on the adventure of his life, encountering exploding museums, train derailments and chaos galore everywhere he goes.

Bronze Medal winner for Best Regional Fiction (Canada-West) at the Independent Publisher Book Awards!

Follow my adventures at www.snookbooks.com

Printed in Canada